THE
RAVEN
HEIR

THE
RĀVEN
HEIR

STEPHANIE BURGIS

BLOOMSBURY
CHILDREN'S BOOKS
LONDON OXFORD NEW YORK NEW DELHI SYDNEY

BLOOMSBURY CHILDREN'S BOOKS
Bloomsbury Publishing Plc
50 Bedford Square, London WC1B 3DP, UK
29 Earlsfort Terrace, Dublin 2, Ireland

BLOOMSBURY, BLOOMSBURY CHILDREN'S BOOKS and the Diana
logo are trademarks of Bloomsbury Publishing Plc

First published in Great Britain in 2021 by Bloomsbury Publishing Plc

A catalogue record for this book is available from the British Library

ISBN: PB: 978-1-5266-1444-5; eBook: 978-1-5266-1442-1

2 4 6 8 10 9 7 5 3 1

Typeset by RefineCatch Limited, Bungay, Suffolk

Printed and bound in Great Britain by CPI Group (UK) Ltd, Croydon CR0 4YY

To find out more about our authors and books visit www.bloomsbury.com
and sign up for our newsletters

For Ollie and Jamie Samphire.
I love you both exactly equally

'Are not these woods more free from peril than the envious court?'

– William Shakespeare, As You Like It

1

Beyond the castle's moat, the deep, dark forest was shot through with trails of sunlight, tracing golden paths of possibility. Robins sang from hidden branches while swifts dived and darted over the sun-dappled water. They were all wild with the first taste of summer, and so was the dark-haired girl who sat, bare feet dangling against stone, on the windowsill of her tower bedroom, watching them fly.

Inside the castle, her mother and her older brother, Connall, were busy in the herbarium as usual, casting stinking enchantments to protect their home against the world. Cordelia's triplet sister, Rosalind, was loudly bashing mock enemies in the first inner courtyard, using the latest long stick that she'd adopted as a sword. Their triplet brother, Giles, strummed a lute soulfully in his tower bedroom high above, windows left open to spread his endless wailing song through the warm air.

But outside the castle, the birds were free, and so could Cordelia be, if only—

No! Catching herself leaning forward, she forced herself to stop before wings could sprout from her back.

She couldn't turn bird and fly out into the sunshine. *Not today.* She'd promised Mother never to do it again without Connall's supervision, even though that was a *ridiculous* rule. It meant only going out once or twice a week, when she wanted to fly free every day. They lived all alone in the centre of an enchanted forest. Who could possibly hurt her among the trees? And why would they want to?

But those were questions that Mother would never answer, like everything else about their family's past … and the last time Cordelia had given in to temptation and flown free on her own for one delicious, stolen afternoon, Mother had cast a cloud of dark smoke to wrap tightly around her window for an entire week in punishment. So Cordelia only sighed and tipped her head back now to soak in the gorgeous warmth of the sunshine on her face and the vast, familiar murmuring of the deep forest around her …

Until harsh voices called out suddenly in the distance.

She jerked upright, eyes flying open. No animals in the forest made sounds like that! Sixteen-year-old Connall's voice was the closest she could think of – but even his wasn't nearly so deep.

'Mother?' she whispered.

If her mother had been paying attention, she would have heard that whisper through the tug of connection that she'd laid upon all her children. Spellcasting must have taken all her focus, though, for Cordelia still sat, uncertain and unanswered, on her windowsill a minute later when the first grown men she'd ever seen burst through the trees into the narrow clearing beyond the moat, wearing armour that clanked and flashed in the sunlight.

'There!' The first one strode forward, as big and hulking himself as the raging bear painted on his shield. A great black beard jutted out beneath his iron helmet. 'The sorceress's castle – and no dragons guarding the gate after all!'

'None that we've seen … *yet*.' The man who answered was lean and poised, like the wolf who snarled on his own shield – and he looked every bit as ready to spring. His head turned, predatory gaze sweeping the clearing. 'We may have slipped past her outer shields with our ploy, but that's no guarantee of our safety from now on.'

Cordelia held her breath, unmoving on her perch, as more and more armoured men and women flooded out of the trees behind the first two. Each of them carried a shield with a wolf or a bear in one hand and a long, sharp-looking sword in the other, and they took up position behind their two leaders.

Too late to change into a bird for safety now! She should have slipped inside before, if only her insatiable curiosity had allowed it. Her feet and arms were nearly as pale as stone, though, and her comfortable old linen gown – carefully ripped along the sides to allow herself proper adventures – was a deep green that matched the ivy on the walls. Perhaps they wouldn't notice her?

'No dragon,' said the leader of the wolf-knights, 'but a little spy watching us with big eyes for her mistress. You, girl!' he called out. 'Tell the Dowager Duchess she has visitors!'

The Dowager Duchess? Cordelia stared at him.

There were no duchesses in their castle. No one lived with their family at all except for Mother's friend Alys, who looked after the goats, argued with Mother over what to plant in the kitchen gardens, and was almost always covered in dirt up to her bony elbows.

On long winter evenings in the great hall, after Giles had finished singing his latest ballads, Mother would often summon up a pile of tiny scented silk-bound books to read out loud to all of them. Cordelia had heard of elegant, powerful duchesses in those pages, along with queens and countesses and fiercely beautiful knights in armour ... but none of them sounded anything like Alys.

'The girl's obviously simple,' said the leader of the bear-soldiers. 'No sense looking for any help there.' Shaking his head, he cupped his big hands around his mouth and bellowed, 'Sorceress, reveal yourself! Or we'll attack!'

Cordelia winced. Mother wasn't going to like that threat at all!

For one long moment, silence hung over the clearing. Even the birds in the forest stopped calling. They were wise enough to hide in times like these.

Then Cordelia *felt* Mother rush towards them through the castle, grabbing out for the whole family at once – not her usual gentle brush against their thoughts, but a hot, frantic swipe.

CORDELIA!

I'm fine! Cordelia hastily pushed her own thoughts back at her mother. **But there are men at the gate. They—**

The great silver portcullis flung itself open, and her mother exploded through it. She was still wearing her stained working apron from the herbarium, and more than half of her long dark hair had twisted free of its constraining plait. But Mother never needed to look tidy to be imposing.

Long weeds from the bottom of the moat shot up and wove themselves together to build a living drawbridge for her to stalk across in fury. Bobbing shapes beneath the green moss and lily pads burst upward as she passed, revealing venomous snakes, long and coiling, heading straight for the invaders. They swam as fast as shadows, and the closest soldiers jumped back, shouting at the sight of them.

I should have thought to change into one of them, Cordelia thought wistfully.

It was too late to hide among the water snakes now. Mother's voice snapped through Cordelia's head as she stalked forward:

Get off that windowsill *now*. Out of sight!

Ugh! Cordelia scrambled back into her bedroom and sank obediently to the floor beneath the window … for a moment. Then she lifted herself just enough to peer outside.

It wasn't as if she was in any danger now that Mother was here. If anyone would simply take the time to *explain*—

'Make way!' A hard push shoved her aside, and Rosalind took her place. 'I want to see!'

6

'Go somewhere else!' Cordelia shoved her hard. 'You've got your own room!'

'But *you've* got the best view.'

'Out of the way, runts!' Giles skidded in behind them, panting, and squeezed his way into the middle. 'I couldn't hear anything from my tower.'

'Not over the sound of your own voice, you mean,' muttered Rosalind.

Cordelia snorted in agreement.

'Shh!' Connall stepped into the room behind them. '*Quiet.*'

It was a spell, not an order; the lips of all three triplets sealed themselves shut against their wills. Cordelia gritted her teeth, Giles sighed through his nose, and Rosalind punched out wildly, her face reddening with rage – but their older brother ignored the blow, leaning over all of them with his gaze intent and his light brown hands braced around Cordelia's windowsill.

Now Cordelia couldn't even see what was happening through her own window! In her family, she could never keep *anything* for herself.

She could still hear their mother's voice, though. '... bellowing at *my* door as if you had *any right* to intrude on my home after all these years?'

'Duchess.' That was the leader of the wolf-knights, his

7

ɔice smoother than his friend's. 'We apologise for the rudeness of our greeting. We fought long and hard to reach your gate, and our manners were strained by the journey.'

'My *patience* has been strained more than enough.' Mother's voice was colder than Cordelia had ever heard it. 'State your business and begone, all of you.'

'Alas, we bring grave news that will not be dismissed so easily,' said the wolf-leader. 'King Edmund – long rest his soul – is dead.'

Cordelia felt Mother's gasp; it was a ripple of unease that billowed through their connection, sending a disconcerting chill through Cordelia's body before Mother snapped her emotions tightly shut, closing herself off from everyone. 'And?' she demanded. 'What has that to do with me?'

'Your game is over, sorceress,' snarled the bear-leader. 'You've lost. You won't hide the heir from us any longer! And if it were up to me, I can tell you—'

'It is time, madam,' interrupted the wolf-leader, 'to return to our kingdom at long last so your child may rule over all of us.'

2

Cordelia knew the taste of secrets. It was the bitterness that coated her tongue each time her mother walked away from another question about the past, why they had to hide inside their castle, and why no other humans were allowed into their forest. Over the years, she'd come up with a thousand different stories to make up for it.

She had never imagined this one.

Connall, a king? Her skin tingled with the thrill of discovery – but Connall's face tightened with visible panic as he stared out of the window at their visitors.

'You're wasting your time here!' His voice hadn't cracked in years, but it cracked now, and his long fingers clenched around Cordelia's windowsill as he leaned forward to shout down at them. 'There's no one here but me and my mother and our servants!'

Servants?

Giles's eyebrows shot up in exaggerated outrage, and Rosalind made a rude gesture at their older brother, but Cordelia's eyes narrowed with suspicion.

Even more secrets.

'Give it up, Lord Connall.' That was the bear-leader, his deep voice dripping with disdain. 'We won't be taken in by any lies. We *know* the babe your mother carried was safely born in this cursed forest. Every seer in the nation agrees.'

Surely no one would speak to their future king that way.

But Connall had a different father from his younger siblings; Cordelia had teased that much out of him years ago. So, if the crown wasn't coming to *him* …

Giles's pale freckled face shone with excitement as he jabbed one finger at his own skinny chest. Of *course* Giles would love to be a king! Then he could force everyone to listen to his songs whether they wanted to or not.

Rosalind shook her head fiercely, pointing at her own chest … and then, shrugging, she pointed to Cordelia.

It was true. None of them knew which had been born first.

It could be any of us.

'I told you years ago,' their mother snapped, 'my family renounces all claim to the Raven Throne. Let it go to any fool who wants it – anyone but *my* children. Take it yourself, for all I care!'

The bear-leader let out a wordless growl. 'If you think—!'

'You may have given up the throne on your children's behalf,' cut in the wolf-leader, 'but – forgive me, madam – they inherit through their father, the late Duke of Harcourt, not through you. His family will *never* allow you to deprive his heirs of their rightful position.'

'*Rightful position?*' Mother's voice rose to a shriek of fury. 'I've seen what happens to the pawns in this battle! The moment my children leave this forest, they'll be targets for every rival to the throne. How many of your great *kings* have ever survived more than a year after their own coronations? And how many—?'

'I'll chop off your head myself before I allow you to steal my cousin's legacy, witch!' the bear-leader bellowed back. 'You'll *never* stop his child from inheriting the throne!'

Arrows flew at his roar, a clap of thunder sounded from Mother's outflung hands in return, and screaming harpies made of ivy launched themselves from the castle walls.

As the scene outside descended into pointless fighting, Cordelia sighed and scooted backwards, leaving her space at the windowsill to her siblings. Over the years, she'd had more than enough experience watching Mother fight off everything from giant rabid bears to the most terrifying magical workings created by Connall in their joint practice-battle sessions.

It wasn't as if human soldiers could offer her any challenge by comparison.

The others shouldered into Cordelia's abandoned space immediately, their eager gazes fixed outside. Rosalind's right arm jerked back and forth, making sword-fighting gestures as if she could implant herself in the battle by sheer force of will. Even Connall was fully focused on the conflict as he leaned over the other two.

So no one noticed when Cordelia shifted into a small brown mouse and skittered across the stone floor, away from them.

Mice were *lovely* for keeping out of sight. Still, they weren't the fastest of creatures, and she was in a hurry. Mother wouldn't take long to send those soldiers packing. As the intruders' shouts of rage turned into fear, Cordelia raced as quickly as she could out of the room and on to the narrow stone platform that overlooked the sunny main courtyard. As soon as she was safely outside, she shifted into a cat, long-legged, sleek and muscular.

Much better! She twitched her dark grey tail with satisfaction and shook out her supple cream-coloured body.

Her pointed ears swivelled, following a soft humming sound in the distance even as distracting scents rose up to call to her sensitive nose from all directions.

There.

She knew that sound. Alys was puttering around the kitchen gardens, humming the tune that Mother had always sung to the children when they were small and needed comfort. If anyone knew the answers Cordelia needed, it would be her ... and if Cordelia got to her while Mother was distracted, she might even admit to some of them.

Springing as a cat felt almost as glorious as flying. Cordelia leaped from the stone platform and landed safely on all four grey paws on the weathered paving stones where Rosalind had practised fighting earlier. The upturned clay urns and broken plants were still there to prove it, along with the discarded sword-stick. Cordelia jumped carefully over her sister's mess, whiskers prickling with distaste, then sped for the ivy-covered stone archway that led towards the second inner courtyard.

There were no hard paving stones here. It had been planted long ago with gardens that filled the air with flavour and drew bees and other insects from the forest. Large chickens bustled about self-importantly, making rounds and clucking loudly as Cordelia prowled through the archway.

The family's three grumpy goats, Honey, Marmalade and Muck, stood chewing and glowering menacingly at Alys as she knelt over the herb beds, still humming to herself. She didn't seem to notice the pointed glares of the goats, the distant shouts of battle, or anything else …

Until Cordelia landed on her wiry back, claws extended, and firmly nuzzled her slim neck.

'Ack!' Herbs scattered everywhere as Alys jerked with shock.

Cordelia *loved* being a cat! She twisted neatly in mid-air as she fell and shifted back into her own human body as she landed on the ground.

'I might have known.' Groaning, Alys scooped up the cut herbs that she'd dropped and deposited them in a large bowl nearby. 'Shouldn't Connall be looking after you, you menace?'

Cordelia pointed at her closed lips.

'Oh, you lot!' Shaking her head, Alys reached into her apron and took out the polished grey river stone that Mother had given her years ago. She touched it lightly to Cordelia's face, then turned back to the herb bed, dropping the stone into her pocket for the next time it was needed.

'Connall's busy,' said Cordelia. She curled her legs on the grass beside Alys and propped herself on one arm with her hand buried in the rich, warm soil of the herb bed. She could almost feel the worms burrowing busily underneath – but she forced herself to cut off that thought immediately.

She could wriggle in worm shape almost any time she wanted. The moment that Mother swept back into the castle, though, her chance to trick anything useful out of Alys would be gone.

'I was just wondering, for no particular reason …' Cordelia tilted her head back and gazed up into the blue sky, as if she had nothing more important to do with her life than stay trapped in one place, only following those shifting white clouds with her eyes. 'Do you happen to remember which of us was born first?'

'Connall,' said Alys. 'Obviously.'

'I *meant* …' She broke off as Alys sat back, lowering dirt-covered hands to her aproned lap and regarding Cordelia with a knowing glint in her green eyes. 'I meant,' Cordelia continued more quietly, 'out of me and Giles and Rosalind.'

'I know.' Alys sighed heavily and scraped a fine strand of red hair back underneath her white cotton coif, leaving a wide stripe of dirt across her pale cheek. 'So. You've been eavesdropping out front, I take it?'

Cordelia frowned mutinously at her. 'How would you know what's been happening out there? It's much too far away to hear any details from here.'

'Trust me,' said Alys, 'I know exactly who's standing at the gate right now, trying to break their way in with sweet words or sharp axes. Your mother and I have been waiting for them for the past twelve years.'

Ever since we were born. Cordelia slid her a sidelong look. '… Because Giles is next in line to be king?'

'Sly one.' Alys's voice was dry. 'You won't catch me out that easily. If you have any questions about your birth, ask your mother.'

'But she never tells me *anything*!' Cordelia's words turned into a muffled yell of frustration as the massive wooden door at the front of the castle slammed shut with an unmistakable thud. The portcullis came crashing down after it.

'There she is, safely back!' Alys's whole body sagged with relief.

Had she actually been worried? About *Mother*?

A smile tugged at Alys's thin lips as she rolled out her shoulders. 'Let's hope Kathryn saw them off properly.'

'Of *course* she did.' As if that had ever been in question! 'But now they'll all slink away – however many of them are left – and then we'll never have any interesting visitors again!'

For one wonderful moment, the world outside their forest had seemed so wide and full of possibilities – as if she could *finally* explode out into it and be free.

Cordelia should have known better than to imagine it could ever really happen.

'Hmm.' Alys rose to her feet, slapping dirt off her rolled-up sleeves. 'For all our sakes, my young eyes and ears, I hope you're right. But if I know the houses of Arden and Lune …' Her face hardened. For one disconcerting moment, Cordelia glimpsed something cold and bleak and shadowed in her eyes – something Cordelia had never seen before in all their years of busy, stifling, jostling family life.

'Now that they've finally found a way into Kathryn's forest,' Alys said softly, 'today will be only the beginning.'

3

There was no time left for asking questions, no matter how many burned inside Cordelia. Mother swept through the castle like a thunderstorm, sending a cloud of impenetrable black smoke around all the outer walls until it covered every window and arrow slit. It was as if she wanted to trap all of them in ignorance of the outside world *forever*!

Cordelia turned herself into a worm and burrowed furiously into the herb garden to eat dirt and seethe in perfect privacy. But she could never avoid her family for long.

'*Mmmm!*'

In worm shape, she had no ears. But the vibrations of a human voice echoed through the warm, dark soil, disrupting everything horribly. Light broke above her, irritating her sensitive skin, and a voice roared all around her: '*Mmmmmm!*'

That *had* to be Giles – and she was in no mood for one of his epic performances. Cordelia wriggled deeper into darkness as quickly as she could.

She wasn't quick enough. He scooped her out a moment later, dirt scattering around her wildly twisting body, and lifted her high into the too-bright air. '*Mmmmmm!*'

Oh, fine. Cordelia shifted into human shape – and landed hard on her hands and knees on the ground as he let her go. '*What?*' Scowling at her triplet brother, she picked herself up and brushed off the green gown that she was once again wearing over her shorter undertunic. 'I do *not* want to hear any songs about what's happened. Go bother Rosalind if you want an audience! All I care about is who those people were.'

'You're in a grumpy mood, aren't you?' Giles grinned down at her. He'd changed clothes since she'd seen him last. Now he was resplendent in his favourite peacock-blue doublet and hose and bouncing up and down on the pointed toes of his shoes as if he might launch into a race at any moment. 'It's supper time,' he told her, 'and you shouldn't have run off like that in the first place. I thought Connall's head would pop off when he saw you were gone! He was convinced you must have thrown yourself into some terrible danger.'

19

'H*mmph*.' Cordelia started towards the main courtyard without waiting for him to follow. 'Connall worries about *everything*,' she said, and Giles wrinkled his nose in rueful agreement.

Unlike the triplets, their older brother obediently followed Mother's lead in every way. He spent hours every day in training to control the natural magic in his blood. He worked with Mother to defend the castle and the forest from any possible attacks, and he worried *endlessly* about everything that might go wrong for everybody in their family. Some of Cordelia's very first memories were of Connall racing to scoop her up with infuriatingly long, strong arms, away from every adventure *he* considered too dangerous.

Now that actual intruders had appeared in real life, he would become *impossible*.

It wasn't that she didn't love him, of course. How could she not? But he could never seem to remember that he *wasn't* an adult yet, not like Mother or Alys. So why couldn't he relax and let himself have some fun? Mother would never have forced him to study magic. She had barely even argued when Giles and Rosalind had decided to give up their own magical training after only a few months of lessons. Cordelia had expected all sorts of ructions and storms – but for once, Mother had taken a rebellion in her stride.

'I'd never force any of you on to my own path,' she had told them all with an uncharacteristic sigh. 'I've learned better than to do that to my own children.'

Unlike Cordelia, Giles and Rosalind had more than enough innate magical potential to change the world with all sorts of different sorceries, as Mother and Connall did every day – but neither of Cordelia's triplets had wanted to spend their lives learning how to manage the magic in their blood. Giles had been singing for as long as Cordelia could remember, and if Mother hadn't agreed to arrange knight lessons, Rosalind would have ended up bashing down half of the castle – *and* both of her triplets along the way! – to let off all her irrepressible physical energy.

As for Cordelia ... well, *her* powers had twisted into their own unique shape long before any of the triplets had grown old enough to train. Even Mother had admitted that it wasn't worth trying to funnel them into any kind of world-affecting sorcery. Cordelia had simply been born wild and half animal – more suited to the woods outside their castle than to any of the comfortable rooms within – and now her breath caught in a jagged gasp of pain as a sudden, intense pang for the freedom outside their walls tugged like a hook inside her chest.

Years of practice at resisting that physical tug kept her feet moving towards those stuffy inner rooms of the castle where she would be trapped for the rest of the night. She couldn't help the snap that pinged through her voice, though, as she answered Giles. 'Why would I stay to watch Mother send them away? They're all gone now, and none of us could have stopped it, so—'

'They're *not* gone.'

Cordelia stopped walking so abruptly that her brother stepped straight into her.

Giles gave a crow of delight as they untangled themselves. 'I *told* you it was silly to leave! You missed a tremendous battle. Rosalind's still trying to make out how all the sword moves work.'

'Of course she is.' Cordelia rolled her eyes. Since she was Rosalind's usual sparring partner, she was likely to experience those moves all too soon. 'But what *happened*?' she demanded. 'How did they escape Mother's creatures?'

'We-e-ell, I wouldn't say they *escaped*,' said Giles. 'I'm working on a whole new ballad about it, though! *They sliced and swished in mighty thwacks—*'

Cordelia gave him one of Alys's best Stern Looks, which all three of the triplets could imitate to perfection. '*N*o singing. Just answer the question!'

'Chi-i-i-ldren!' Alys's voice echoed through the courtyards as if Cordelia had summoned her with the impersonation. 'No more dilly-dallying! Your supper's growing cold!'

Everyone in the castle knew better than to argue with Alys when it came to food. But as they both obediently broke into a run, Cordelia hissed, 'We would've had enough time if it weren't for useless ballads!'

Giles huffed back, '*You* should have listened. It's my best one yet! One day, kings and queens will empty their treasuries to hear me sing.'

Not if I'm the queen! The retort rose automatically to Cordelia's tongue ... but she bit it back instead of tossing the rude words at her brother as usual. That jest felt suddenly too dangerous to make in the open air, where anyone might overhear it.

'Where *are* those soldiers now?' she whispered as they hurried through the open doorway into the buttery, just outside the great hall. She scooped up the leather shoes she had left there after breakfast and slipped them on quickly as she walked. 'Are they hiding in the forest?'

Giles leaned down to breathe his reply into her ear as they swung the big door of the great hall open together. 'No, they're gathered just outside the castle, *right there in the open*. That's why she covered up all the windows when she gave up on chasing them away!'

Gave up? Cordelia's jaw dropped open.

Mother *never* surrendered. Not about anything! A thousand questions swarmed to Cordelia's lips ...

But the door swung open under their hands, and she swallowed down every word as she saw Mother and Alys already sitting at the hulking wooden table ahead with Rosalind and Connall and a steaming cauldron of stew.

When Mother was in a good mood, the whole castle felt as if it had been filled with sunshine, and every member of the family glowed with her vibrant warmth. But when she wasn't …

Head down and lips pressed together, Cordelia took her empty seat next to Connall and prepared to avoid every ominously looming storm cloud. She'd just get through a nice, quiet dinner, and then—

Beaming, Rosalind waved her soup spoon at the rest of the family. She was still dressed in the plain green tunic and woollen leggings that she'd worn for her fighting practice earlier, and her short black hair stuck up around her head in cheerful tufts. 'Isn't it absolutely marvellous? We're under siege! Surrounded by invaders! I can't wait to start boiling oil to pour down on them the next time they attack.'

Cordelia exchanged a look of pure agony across the table with Giles. Would their bullish triplet *never* develop any sensitivity?

Their older brother opened his mouth, wincing, but it was too late for even Connall to turn this storm.

'It is not a *siege!*' Mother slammed one hand on to the

table with a thud that echoed through the hall. 'I refuse to dignify those cockroaches outside with that term.'

This time, Alys winced. 'Kathryn, do remember that one of those *cockroaches* is my brother.'

'*Which one?*' Cordelia mouthed at Giles.

He lifted his shoulders in a shrug.

Alys didn't *look* bearish or wolfish to Cordelia. She was just … Alys, who took turns with Mother in feeding the family, ordering them all around, and ruthlessly trimming Cordelia's long hair whenever it grew too tangled for her to bear the sight of it any longer. She managed all the non-magical practicalities in the castle and was as steady and sensible as a rock.

Cordelia had never realised that Alys was hiding secrets of her own too.

Connall said, 'Perhaps we could find a way to convince—'

'No.' Mother scooped up her silver goblet and took a long swallow. 'I refuse to spend any more of my day discussing those creatures. They can sit outside and rot for the rest of their lives. Eventually they'll tire of it and leave or else they'll die of old age. Either one is fine by me!'

No. Cordelia's fingers clenched around her soup spoon as her chest squeezed tight.

She couldn't stay locked inside forever. She *couldn't*.

But – as usual – no one was asking for her opinion.

'Kathryn …' Alys sighed, her face softening as she looked across the table. 'We've spent the last twelve years in hiding. You know I thought it the wisest solution too – but it hasn't worked after all. They haven't given up – and today, our refuge grew so much smaller and more vulnerable. At least Arden and Lune want the children alive, unlike the Duchess of Solenne or the Dukes of Breville or Mordaunt. For all we know, *they* might arrive next. Don't you think it's finally time to compromise?'

Mother gave a bitter laugh. 'Which of my children would you sacrifice to that *compromise*, dear friend? Rosalind? Giles? Cordelia?' She gestured to each of them in turn, her dark eyes shining with an angry glitter that looked impossibly like tears. 'They wouldn't last a month at court, and you know it.'

'I would so!' Rosalind scowled ferociously. 'Anyone who tried to attack *me*—'

'I'd quite *like* to be king,' said Giles. 'I'll wager kings can have as many lutes as they like, and no one tells *them* to stop practising, no matter how late it might be. Besides—'

'You two have no idea what you're talking about,' Mother snapped. 'This conversation is over. You will *all* stay safely inside until I tell you otherwise, no matter how long that may take – and we won't speak of this again.'

'No!' The word burst out of Cordelia's mouth like an animal breaking free. She gripped her wooden spoon with all her might, forcing herself not to give in under the weight of Mother's gaze. She had a storm of her own whirling inside now, and it wouldn't let her stop. 'Of course we don't understand,' she said, 'so, tell us! Who *are* those men outside? Which one is Alys's brother? Why do those other dukes and duchesses want us dead? And why won't you ever just *explain* anything?'

Mother's eyes narrowed. 'I don't care for your tone of voice, Cordelia.'

'She's right, though.' Unexpectedly, Connall spoke up beside her, frowning. 'They are getting older, Mother. They have a right to understand, so they can—'

'I can help you fight them off!' Rosalind said eagerly. 'Just point me at them. I'll take down that big one first with my sword like – *thwack!*' Her spoon hit her bowl with a crash that sent stew splashing everywhere.

'*Enough!*' Mother pushed back her chair in a sudden jerky movement that scraped its legs loudly against the flagstones. 'Can't I even eat supper in peace? *There's* my reward for spending all these years trying to protect my family!' Her voice broke in a sudden harsh crack on her last word.

'Mother!'

'Wait!'

Connall and Giles both started from their chairs, reaching towards her, but she strode out of the room without a backwards look, her long green skirts swishing furiously around her.

Alys waved the two boys back into their seats as the big wooden door slammed shut. 'Let her cool her head. She'll calm down soon enough. She's only agitated by the day's events … as we all are.'

Her gaze turned inwards, and her pale eyelids fell to hood her cool green eyes. Cordelia could almost feel the weight of secrets and memories simmering behind them, only a few feet away but hopelessly out of reach.

Just like always.

No one would ever tell her the truth.

Even Alys wasn't reliable any more.

And Mother wanted them all to sit locked inside these castle walls for *years*?

Wings burst open inside Cordelia's chest as the future closed in around her. Her breath turned into ragged, painful pants. She bent over, gasping for air.

She was trapped. She was *caged*. She couldn't breathe! She—

'Cordy?' Rosalind's voice broke through her spiralling panic. 'What's the matter with you?'

'I have to go!' She lurched out of her seat.

She was a mouse an instant later, racing across the flag-stones on all four paws while her unused soup spoon clattered to the floor behind her. The voices of her family shouted after her in protest, but she only ran faster in response. As she reached the end of the hall, one of Connall's rehumanising bolts speared through the air towards her – but she darted out of the way just in time. It hit the flagstones beside her vulnerable tail with a fizzle of disappointment.

She wriggled underneath the closed wooden door, through the buttery, and out into the paved courtyard as loud footsteps sounded behind her. She couldn't stay a moment longer. Not in that room, and not in this big stone trap, either.

Turning cat, she fled across the courtyard, through the archway that led to the kitchen gardens. They lay empty of people and interference and rules, richly scented with growing herbs in the cool, violet air of twilight.

As she leaped through the archway, she *changed*.

Wings beat hard. She launched herself into the open sky, an insignificant brown bird like dozens of others in the big green forest. No one would notice her, she was sure. No one would care even if they did. But she was free and unchained. She would never allow herself to be trapped …

29

And as she rose above the castle in swift form, she curved a wide arc through the air to aim herself at those mysterious encampments beyond the smoke-shrouded front walls.

Mother would never willingly share any secrets – so Cordelia would simply find them out herself.

4

Seen through a swift's eyes, the world always expanded, exploding with new shades of colour. This time, though, it had all changed – and it looked so *wrong* that it hurt Cordelia's stomach.

As she winged over the castle's high watchtowers, she saw gap after gap ahead where ancient trees had stood for all her life until now. The first few rows past the moat had all been felled and brutally stripped of the branches and leaves where birds had nested and sung earlier that day.

Some of those long trunks had been stacked to form a set of makeshift walls around two central groups of tents. Others had been chopped up to build campfires that sent trails of hot smoke high into the sky. Each fire sat between another cluster of the smaller cloth tents that lined the enlarged clearing, with tall wolf or bear flags planted by each one.

Even more trees had been slaughtered beyond the tents, then left carelessly abandoned with broken nests and shattered eggs lying on the ground nearby.

If she'd had Mother's powers, Cordelia would have attacked. But swifts couldn't rain down magical vengeance upon anyone. The only thing Cordelia could ever control with magic was her own shape – and even now, her tiny flying body was driven by an irresistible need to explore and understand *everything*.

So she bottled up her outrage and dived, silent and graceful, over the rippling moat, where snakes bobbed watchfully and the water was flecked to swift-sight with dots of hours-old blood. It beckoned to her – *Come, sip on the wing!* – but she fought the instinct and only nabbed an insect in mid-air.

Stashing it in the back of her throat, she landed on the ground beyond the moat and hopped awkwardly forward on her three-clawed feet towards the closest fire and the big men who surrounded it. They sat with their massive backs to her, rumbling to each other in words she wasn't close enough to understand.

Slowly, quietly …

Cordelia forced herself to stop and peck pointlessly at

the ground every few moments, just in case anyone was watching, while all the other birds hid in the trees, out of sight.

The whole forest felt as if it were holding its breath.

Closer … Closer … Almost there …

That was when everything went wrong.

Today's attack really had made Connall impossible.

He slammed open the front door and portcullis of their smoke-enveloped castle. Black and purple shadows swirled wrathfully around his lanky figure, which stood utterly alone in defiance of all Mother's orders.

'Cordy! Get back here, now!' he bellowed as soldiers leaped to their feet all along the banks of the moat.

He made a quick, twisting gesture with one hand. A tunnel of tightly funnelled air formed before him, visible to birds but not to humans. It offered a safe passage across the water, perfectly shaped for one small brown swift to fly through, protected from arrows or any other attacks … just as Cordelia had been forced back to safety at least a hundred times before by his long arms and overprotective spells.

Why did he *always* have to interfere with her adventures? Snarling inwardly, Cordelia hopped away as his searching gaze swept the clearing. The men by the fires were all shouting loudly. She would hide behind their big bodies until he gave up, and then—

Her older brother's voice slammed into her ears, magically directed this time and loud enough to make her flinch. **Now, Cordelia! Don't make me get Mother to drag you back. *If* you come now, I won't tell her what you were up to.**

Ugh! Cordelia spread out her wings in furious preparation to launch back towards her ridiculous brother, who *never* trusted her to look after herself.

Lightning cracked across the moat beneath the cloudless sky. It came from the clearing full of soldiers.

There were sorcerers among the invaders too.

If that lightning had struck Connall's shifting cape of shadows, it would have bounced aside without harm. Cordelia had seen it repel magical attacks before, when Connall had practised it with Mother in their courtyard. But this sorcerer wasn't aiming at Connall … and apparently, when Connall had come running to save his sister, he hadn't expected anyone behind him to need a shield.

The lightning shot over his head and through the arch of the open doorway.

A terrible scream sounded inside.

'A*lys!*'

It was Connall who shouted her name, whirling

34

around, but Cordelia screamed too as she flung herself into the air.

... *Too late!* The safe tunnel of air her older brother had shaped vanished the moment that his concentration broke.

Black arrows shot in a murderous cloud across the moat, their steady *thwack* ... *thwack* ... *thwack*s filling the air with an inescapable percussion. Connall's back was still turned, blocking the sight of whatever was happening inside their home. Arrows bounced off his shifting cape and off the smoke-wrapped stone walls of the castle, showering into the moat as snakes hissed and dived for cover. No one even noticed Cordelia's small brown body amidst the chaos, flying frantically back and forth as she searched for any possible angle of approach.

Archers lined the banks of the moat. Even bird-sight wasn't powerful enough to find a way through their combined attack.

'Why would you ever take such a risk?' Connall shouted at their invaders. Cordelia couldn't see him any more through the cloud of arrows, but she could hear him, and his voice was choked with horrifying tears. 'You may hate me and my mother, my lord Duke of Arden, but *that's your sister* who was struck just now!'

'Rubbish!' The bear-leader stomped out of the central

cluster of tents with a young squire scurrying after him, still fastening the last plates of armour around his enormous chest. 'I have no sister any more. Even if I *had*, Alys was raised in a fortress. She'd never be fool enough to stand so close to—'

'What have you done?' Mother burst past Connall through the door, throwing out her arms to create a transparent bubble of protection that no arrow could pierce. 'You shot a lethal curse into our home?'

Scowling, Arden crossed his arms with a clank of armour. 'Lune? What nonsense is she spouting now?'

'There is no need to fear, Duchess.' The wolf-leader, already fully armoured, had been standing on the other side of the bank, but he held out his hands now in a signal that finally halted that steady shower of arrows.

As the archers lowered their bows, Cordelia's whole body jerked with the instinct to seize the moment and fly through the open air. But her mother's bubble was too strong. It would hold her out too.

And she needed to hear the answer to this question.

The wolf-leader scooped off his helmet and held it out before him like a peace offering. 'We have the spellcaster right here,' he said, 'only waiting to remove the curse that she laid. You know we would never choose to cause irreversible harm to anyone. All you need do is *ask* us to heal whichever poor soul bore the brunt of this unnecessary battle ... A battle, I might add, that was brought about by your own treasonous choices.'

'All I need do is ask?' Mother's voice was flat with disbelief. 'And what exactly will happen if I *do* ask for your help in saving my dearest friend's life?'

'Why, then,' said the wolf-leader, 'we will be more than happy to enter your home and instruct our caster to reverse her curse, healing your friend completely ... the very moment you surrender to us.'

'I don't understand. How could this have *happened*?' Mother's strong voice wavered for the first time in Cordelia's memory. 'How was this door even opened in the first place? Connall, if they attacked, why didn't you call me to deal with them?'

Connall didn't reply out loud. But a moment later, Cordelia shook in mid-air with the gale of her mother's voiceless reaction.

CORDELIA!

She had expected the blast of fury that shot through their connection. She'd braced herself for it. But she had never expected the terror that accompanied it.

Mother wasn't ever supposed to feel fear.

'Mother,' Connall said, 'if we don't let them in, Alys will *die*.'

Mother looked across the moat at Cordelia's small hovering body, past the line of archers. She looked back inside. Then she closed her eyes.

Run. Her silent order shot through the family's connection, calling to all three triplets at once. **Run as fast and as far as you can. Giles, Rosalind, take the tunnel out the back. Meet Cordelia in the trees behind the castle.** *Now!*

Stay safe, stay together, and stay far from sight. I'll come for you as soon as I can. I swear it.

I love you all so much.

Her shoulders slumped. She opened her eyes … and then, as Cordelia stared in disbelief, she sank to her knees before the invaders.

'Very well,' she said out loud. 'The siege has ended.

5

There were no human words in Cordelia any more. She wheeled away from her family's castle and the soldiers flooding into it with no rational thoughts left in her mind. Only flight.

She opened her beak and screamed a wordless swift-scream as she dived into the shadows between the trees, ready to lose herself within them.

But the trees pressed much too close together. Their sweeping, tangling branches slowed her down. She couldn't fly nearly fast enough to take away the pain. So she dropped to the ground and turned fox instead. Then she *ran*. She needed the burn in her muscles. She needed the lunge, and the pounce, and the bite.

So she *caught*, again and again – but then she couldn't eat her prey. Her stomach burned and twisted each time that she sensed their panic. Again and again, she let them go with high, sharp barks of frustration.

Her world was scent. It was rage. It was fear. It was …

Scent! She knew those scents. Two of them, so familiar and so *hers* that they pulled her towards them through the trees before she could even remember what they meant. Until …

'It's her! I told you she'd be running wild.' It was a girl's voice. *Family. Sister.*

Irritating. But Cordelia didn't flinch or back away when the girl's strong fingers closed in the thick fur at her nape, anchoring her in place. The boy fell to his knees beside her a moment later and wrapped his arms tightly around her back and chest. His face tipped, wetness trickling through her coat.

'Come on!' said the girl. 'Hurry up and turn human!'

'Not yet,' said the boy. 'Just one more minute.' He hugged Cordelia even closer.

She should have twisted to free herself, like any sensible fox. Instead, she found herself leaning into him for no reason she could understand. A low whimper escaped her throat, although her body felt no pain.

'Oh—!' The girl let go of Cordelia and swung around, bashing the closest branch hard with the long stick that she carried.

'Quiet!' The boy jerked upright. 'We can't make any noise!'

Giles was complaining about noise?

It was no good. With her triplets bickering around her, there was no way for Cordelia to hide from reality any longer. An inescapable wave of memories and awful, helpless humanness broke through her wild foxness like a dam shattering.

She shifted. Giles's arm fell away as she straightened, kneeling on the bumpy forest floor and breathing hard. 'How long has it been?' Her voice sounded hoarse.

She'd screamed in swift form, hadn't she? That would explain why her throat hurt now. She couldn't remember much that had happened since that moment when …

When …

'Too long. You were supposed to come right here, remember?' Rosalind smacked her stick irritably against one leg, peering around the gathering darkness suspiciously. 'We could have started out half an hour ago, if you'd only been waiting where you were supposed to be.'

'We wouldn't be here at all if she ever stayed where she was *supposed* to be,' Giles muttered.

At that, the urge to run – again – rose up within her in a surging wave, trying to propel her to her feet. Cordelia's hands clenched into fists on her knees, holding herself down. 'Is Alys all right?'

'Who knows?' Giles's fingers rattled against his side, playing an invisible, agitated tune. He'd followed Mother's orders, she saw; not a single lute strap hung over his shoulder. How he must have hated leaving all of them behind. 'Haven't you felt it?'

'Felt what?'

'Try talking to Mother,' Rosalind told her.

'But—'

'*Do it!*'

Cordelia reached out in her mind. She felt ... nothing. *Emptiness.*

She sucked in a harsh breath.

'You see?' Rosalind's knuckles whitened around her stick. 'She's gone.'

Goosebumps popped across Cordelia's arms. 'What do you mean, *gone*?'

'They did something to her,' Giles said. 'They haven't killed her. They *couldn't* have. We would have felt it if they had! But they've stopped her magic somehow. We can't reach her, and she can't reach us either.'

'And we didn't even try to protect her!' Rosalind whirled around, lashing out with her stick and sending leaves scattering to the ground from nearby branches. 'She wouldn't let me help, and I was stupid enough to *listen*. Now, all because I was a coward—'

'What could you have done?' Uncontrollable shivers rippled through Cordelia's skin. 'That stick of yours can't stop magical lightning.'

That terrible scream …

Alys is all right. She has to be. They've healed her.

Cordelia's sister glowered at her. '*You* didn't listen when Mother said to stay back.'

'And look where it got us!' Giles pointed an accusing finger in the direction of home. 'Now Mother's a prisoner. They have Connall and Alys. And they'll come hunting for the three of us next!'

Cordelia flinched.

Rosalind dug her stick hard into the ground. 'Connall told them we were only servants. Remember?'

'But they knew he was lying.' Giles gave a groan of frustration. 'We're the reason they came! They're not going to give up just because we didn't wait for them at the gates. How are we supposed to stop them from taking us when they do come? With your pretend sword? Or one of my ballads?' He snorted, his shoulders hunching and his head ducking down. 'It's absurd.'

'So what are you saying?' Rosalind's eyes narrowed. 'You want to give up without a fight? Surrender?'

'Mother did.' Giles's hands clenched and unclenched in the shadows. 'How are we supposed to fight them if she couldn't?'

'She didn't want us to fight.' Cordelia's throat felt full of pebbles. 'She told us to run.'

… Just before she'd sunk to her knees. 'I *love you all so much.*'

Cordelia knew how to be furious at her mother, but she didn't know how to carry all the feelings that roiled inside her now. They were too big and complicated. They *hurt.*

'I'm not running from anyone,' snarled Rosalind. 'I'm going to rescue Mother and Alys and Connall too.'

'Don't be an idiot!' Giles's voice rose to a whisper-shout. 'This isn't a ballad, and you're not a real knight! You've only ever fought Mother's practice-shadows. Real people are different! And you ran just as fast as I did through that tunnel to get away.'

'I *know* I did.' Rosalind looked away, her voice thickening. 'I can't bear to remember it.'

'*What* tunnel?' Cordelia scowled up at both of them. 'Mother never showed me any tunnels under the moat.'

'Well …' Rosalind wiped her nose with the back of her hand and sniffed hard. 'Of course she didn't. She's not a fool.'

'She showed *us* because she knew we wouldn't use it unless we had to,' Giles said impatiently. 'She didn't dare show *you* because you would've used it to sneak out every time you got tired of following the rules. None of us can ever trust you to stay put!'

If he had *any idea* how hard she'd fought to follow those stupid, suffocating rules – to sit trapped inside the castle's walls on *so many* days when the sky rose high and wild above her and that hook tugged piercingly hard inside her chest …

The need to shift was a wail within her bones as Cordelia surged to her feet, glaring at her brother. 'I'm trying,' she said, 'to follow Mother's rules *right now*. She said to stay out of sight until she comes for us.'

'But what if she can't?' His shoulders sagged as if all the fury had drained out of him, leaving him limp. 'Just … think about it, both of you. We're in the middle of the forest. We don't even have anything to eat – and those men came to make one of us their king or queen! I know Mother didn't want it to happen, but … wouldn't it be the easiest way to *make* them let her go?'

Rosalind's shoulders squared, and she set her jaw. 'It would be a betrayal of Mother's honour for us to turn ourselves in without a fight – especially after she fought so valiantly on our behalf!'

'We're not doing *anything* that those dukes want,' growled Cordelia.

The bearish Duke of Arden didn't even care for his own family. How could he be trusted with anything else? He'd cast aside strong, kind Alys as if she were of no value.

Families argued, but you couldn't just pretend that they didn't *matter*.

She'd already had one brother be taken captive, and the pain of that thought made her breath turn ragged and her head spin as remembered moments flashed past her in vivid accusation. Connall had tried *so hard* to protect her …

She wouldn't let either of her triplets throw themselves away now.

'We can't just go running in with sticks to rescue Mother and the others,' Cordelia told Rosalind. '*They* have real swords – and we don't even understand what's happening.'

If only any of the adults back home had *ever* answered any of her questions!

'What are we going to do, then?' Giles wrapped his arms around his skinny chest. He looked already defeated – and smaller too, without his usual swagger.

It felt wrong to see exuberant Giles so cowed. He should be dancing around composing epic songs about their adventures, not crumpling into himself like a tree ready to topple. Rosalind stood fiercely on guard, which was normal … but the pale fear and guilt on her face felt horribly off-kilter too. Rosalind was always supposed to be absurdly overconfident, no matter how wrong she might actually be.

Everything had fallen apart tonight … and it was all her fault.

But she wasn't going to let herself think about that, *ever*. Instead, she said, 'Everyone needs rest so we can think. I know a den nearby that's empty. Connall and I found it last time I went exploring. You'll both be safe enough sleeping in there.'

'What about you?' Rosalind frowned. 'We'll need to take turns standing guard.'

'No one will get past me tonight.' It was the one thing Cordelia could still be sure of.

It was a relief to turn bear a few minutes later. She stretched her big brown bulk across the entrance to the abandoned wolf den, forming a breathing wall of fur and claws between the wide-open outside world and the tiny, squabbling pieces that remained of her family.

It was her job to protect them now.

It was all that she had left.

Shadows fell across her closed eyelids. Cool night air ruffled through her fur. Owls hooted softly to each other overhead, while mice and pine martens skittered through the thick undergrowth nearby.

She was as free and unleashed as she had ever yearned to be.

And she was so lucky that a powerful wild bear couldn't cry … even when the girl inside had just had her entire world shattered.

6

Cordelia turned bird again at dawn, taking flight in the morning chill before her grumpy, yawning triplets could even think to argue. She left them stumbling through the undergrowth, foraging for wild garlic and berries, kicking aside tangled obstacles and peering sceptically at every plant they saw.

She'd nabbed three spiders before she'd even left the ground. Now her striped wings whirred, and her tiny fire-crest body darted with ease between every leaf-heavy branch, drawn through the forest by a pull stronger than hunger.

The walls of the castle had sung to her veins all night. She wouldn't get too close now – she would be good; she would follow Mother's orders – but she had to see them for herself in bright daylight.

She had to *know*.

What if Mother and Connall had turned out the invaders but couldn't call to the triplets from so far away? What if—?

A stick cracked sharply just ahead. Her body froze in mid-air, wings whirring as she hovered.

That sound hadn't been made by a forest animal.

Neither was the curse that sounded after it.

'Quiet!' hissed a woman's voice. It wasn't Mother or Alys. It came from a knight without armour, creeping between the trees ahead with a quiver of arrows over her back. She carried a long, slender bow in one hand, and her tunic bore the image of a snarling wolf.

She belonged with the smooth-talking Duke of Lune.

The man beside her wore a bear on his tunic, the angry Duke of Arden's symbol, and he growled at her like a bear himself. 'I couldn't help it. By my oath, that stick reached out and tripped me!'

'Remember what Their Graces told us,' she murmured. 'This forest has belonged to the sorceress for years. We can't trust anything we see or hear – and we can't let anything hear *us*. Be a shadow, or we'll never find them.'

'There are too many shadows here already for my liking.' His hand tightened around the vicious-looking spear that he carried ... but at another look from his companion, he lowered it with an angry huff of air. 'They'll come running home soon enough on their own,' he muttered. 'What kind of witch-child could survive in *this* forest?'

The woman shrugged, a sneer twisting at her lips. 'Does it really matter? Your Duke of Arden may declaim all he likes about family loyalty, but we *both* know our lords will run the kingdom for themselves while our new king or queen is a child – and none of these children will live long enough to take control. Like it or not, the Duchess of Solenne and her allies will find some way to kill them off, sooner or later, in favour of her chosen heir. Then we'll kill hers, and on and on it will go. But for now ...'

Her teeth flashed in a predatory smile. 'We need a royal body to stick on to that throne and keep our own masters in charge for as long as possible. So, let's hunt down our next glorious king or queen of Corvenne and get them to the Hall of Investiture whether they like it or not!'

Oh, no, you don't! Cordelia twisted in mid-air and shot back through the trees.

Giles and Rosalind had already wandered too far from the safety of the den – and they weren't even trying to be quiet. She could hear them from yards away, stomping and spitting out experiments.

'Ugh! Leave that one for the—ow!' Rosalind jerked back as Cordelia zoomed towards her and began to tug on Rosalind's short hair with her beak. 'Stupid bird! I don't *want* to steal your food. I—'

'Cordy?' Giles spun around, eyes sharp.

She couldn't bear to shift. Humans were too *slow*! She danced with impatience in the air as she circled them, trying to herd them away.

'Something's wrong,' Giles said.

Finally! They understood.

Rosalind grabbed for her sword-stick and planted her feet wide apart in defence position.

'Argh!' Cordelia let out a muffled shriek of frustration as she landed on two human feet in front of her stupid, stubborn sister. 'Go, go, go! *Don't* stay and fight!'

That bear-man was twice Rosalind's height, at least. And that hard, focused look in the wolf-woman's eyes …

'Where?' Giles looked around, eyes wide. 'The den?'

'Too far!' They would never get there in time.

If only her triplets could shift bodies too! She would have given anything to fly away with them now. Instead, she pointed desperately towards the east. 'There's a fallen oak that tumbled down in the last storm. Go and hide under its leaves. *Now.*'

Rosalind's eyes blazed. '*I'm* not afraid of any—'

'Protect Giles!' Cordelia hissed.

Giles's jaw dropped open in outrage. 'What?'

'You can write a song about it,' she promised. '*Later*.'

She couldn't wait any longer. She dropped into wolf form and ran from her triplets, straight in the direction of the knights creeping towards them.

They were still out of sight, but they weren't out of scent. In wolf form, she could smell the fear and aggravation that pulsed off them in waves – and the determination too. A mere howl in the distance wouldn't frighten these predators away.

The fur on her back rose. Her upper lip lifted in a snarl.

She was a predator now too. They were coming for her *pack*.

The wolf knew exactly what to do.

Her world was made of infinite shades of grey and instinct like a guiding star. Her paws left no imprint on the ground as she sped unerringly through the trees towards her prey.

Closer, closer—

There.

Just ahead. Two humans, stopping to confer.

Her back legs sank down into a crouch. Her whole body prepared to spring.

They turned together.

She *leaped*.

She wasn't aiming to attack. Her fierce bark was a warning any animal would recognise: *Stay away!* Even the fiercest bear or wild boar would take the hint and back away.

But the man lunged forward instead, his sharp spear arcing towards her neck …

And the tip of the woman's arrow sliced through Cordelia's side, sending her spinning and tumbling through the air.

It hurt *so much*! She barely heard the piercing howl of pain that erupted from her throat.

She landed hard on the ground. The man took a quick stride to follow her—

And Giles's voice sang out from twenty feet away. 'Hey! Over here! Aren't you looking for us?'

What was he *doing*? Cordelia fought to pull herself upright. She had to stop the knights from finding him and Rosalind, no matter what it took …

But both of the knights were already running, following Giles's voice through the trees as it rose, high and mocking. 'Can't you even hear me? Over here!'

Cordelia whimpered as she dragged herself to her feet. The rich scent of blood filled her nostrils. The knights had disappeared into the trees. Pain stretched jaggedly through her side as she stumbled heavily after them.

'Cordy, stop!' It was Rosalind who hissed just behind her and Rosalind's hand that grasped the fur around her neck to halt her when Cordelia tried to keep on moving anyway …

But Giles caught up with them only a moment later. 'It's all right, Cordy! I'm here! I'm safe, and it worked. I *did* it!' He let out a laugh of shocked delight.

At the same moment, in the distance – *much* further than before – his voice sang out again, turning high and plaintive. 'Isn't anyone there? We're so helpless! We can't protect ourselves! Won't anybody come and save us?'

Cordelia shook her head hard, trying to make sense of it. None of her senses matched up any more … and her brother sounded like a fool!

'Good news,' Rosalind told her gruffly. 'Giles figured out how to control his magic all on his own.'

'… And it was my greatest performance yet,' Giles finished with deep satisfaction.

7

Shaking her head at both of them, Rosalind peered down at the wet, matted fur around Cordelia's arrow wound. 'Too bad *you* didn't figure out how to fight at the same time. What were you thinking, attacking two armed knights without any training?'

It was *too much*. Cordelia shifted back into her own body with a growl of fury that turned into a horrible moan of pain. She couldn't help curling tightly around the wound in her side, but she glared up fiercely at her rough-handed sister from the ground. 'I was trying to protect you two! If you had only let me …'

Her head spun, horribly. She let it fall against the moss as she mumbled, 'I thought you two didn't do magic any more.'

They hadn't for years, as a point of principle, ever

since they'd forced their way free from Mother's early lessons to choose their own paths in life – and the most that Cordelia had seen from either of them even in those few months of study was levitating a salt cellar or two at the supper table.

'Apparently, that magic in our blood has been growing along with us, even though I didn't pay it any attention until now.' Giles sank down beside her, sickly pale, and summoned up a rueful smile when she looked up at him. 'Mother always said it ought to be all or nothing if we wanted to be proper mages, and I never wanted the kind of training Connall had … but when I heard you scream, I panicked – and the magic just exploded out of me, casting my voice exactly where I wanted it. It's as if it was waiting all along for me to finally remember it was there – or to really, desperately *need* it.'

'*Where are you? We're right here! Won't you even try to find us?*' Quieter and further away with every moment, his other voice receded into the distance.

'How long can you keep it going?' Rosalind asked as she tugged firmly at the arm Cordelia used to hide her wound.

'I don't know.' Giles sighed, drawing his knees up to his chin. 'That's the problem with not having enough training – I don't know how to tell how much strength I've really got. Enough to get us away from here, I think, if I push myself … but you'd better figure out first whether we can safely move her.'

'Ugh!' Giving up, Cordelia pressed her eyes shut, let Rosalind push aside her arm, and buried her face against the damp, mossy ground.

Giles hummed anxiously beside her while their sister pushed up her bloodied but untorn gown and undertunic and prodded at Cordelia's burning wound.

'It doesn't look *too* bad,' Rosalind finally said. 'Connall could sort it out easily enough if he were here.' She sighed. '*We'll* need a bandage, though.'

Giles snorted softly. 'You can't turn yourself into one of those, can you, Cordy?'

Cordelia didn't even bother to roll her eyes at the weak joke. Her own abilities had stayed the same ever since the first time she'd shifted into a bird and flown away from the mashed-up dinner of beets that Alys had been trying to force upon the three of them as infants.

She wished that she had stayed wolf now, so she could run and hide in a burrow to pant out the pain in privacy. It felt even harder to bear in human form, especially with Giles and Rosalind now *both* pushing their fingers around the wound. She gritted her teeth tightly together, breathing through the stabs.

Cloth ripped behind her. A moment later, she felt it being wrapped like a wide belt around her waist.

'Please tell me that didn't come from anybody's under-garments,' she mumbled into the moss.

'Only your undertunic – which was dirty enough.' Rosalind sighed. 'We should've cleaned your wound too, if we had a well out here.'

'There's a stream,' Cordelia mumbled. 'It's not too far away.'

She didn't move, though. Moving would *hurt*.

'Or ...' Giles let out a deep breath as he stood. 'We *could* just surrender to them and let their healers treat you. If we tell them that they have to—'

'No.' Cordelia pushed herself up on to her hands and knees, panting through the agony of the movement. A wild pulse beat against her throat; all her senses felt raw and over-loaded. 'You didn't hear what they were talking about,' she said fiercely, 'but I did – and I can tell you, they don't mean us to survive. We're only puppets to them, to keep their own dukes in power for as long as possible. Arden and Lune are planning to run the country themselves. They won't listen to a word we say – and we'll be dead long before we're grown.'

'What?' Giles's jaw dropped open. 'But—'

'There's no time to talk it over.' Rosalind jumped to her feet, her fists clenching and unclenching by her raggedly torn tunic. 'Those knights are bound to circle back here eventually, once Giles's magic runs out. Let's get moving and find Cordy's stream *right now*.'

Unfortunately, that stream wasn't as close as it should have been. Or was it? Cordelia kept losing track of the space around her as she forced herself along the bumpy, mossy ground, balancing every other step on her sister's long sword-stick and breathing through the pain. Time blurred around her, stretching off into unexpected directions.

Alys's green eyes hardening in the quiet herb garden. '*If* I *know the houses of Arden and Lune* …'

Black smoke sweeping around their windows …

Mother sinking to her knees …

'Look out!' Giles grabbed her free arm.

Cordelia shook off his hand with an irritable grunt. Rosalind was stronger, though, and she grabbed the collar of Cordelia's gown, yanking her backwards. Cordelia's gaze finally cleared and skidded downward as she slipped on the muddy ground and …

There was the stream at last. She had nearly stepped into it.

'We need to clean out that wound, *now*,' said Giles.

Cordelia rolled her eyes. 'I'm not delirious,' she said with dignity. 'I was just *thinking*.'

'Ha,' said Rosalind. 'That'd be a first.'

Gritting her teeth, Cordelia lowered herself carefully to the ground. The pain was good for one thing, at least. It distracted her from the annoyance of her triplets.

She'd thought that the wound had stopped bleeding by then, but once they unwound – and horribly unstuck – the makeshift bandage, it opened up and bled more, after all, into the cold, clear water that the other two splashed over her. They cleaned the ragged bandage too, soaking it in the stream before squeezing it out and wrapping it back around her waist, then tightening it so much that she gasped. Between her wet, cold-pebbled skin and the deep burn of the wound, her balance swooped off and disappeared entirely. She staggered as she pushed herself upright, and when Rosalind grabbed her arm this time, she didn't protest.

'Lie down, *now*,' said her sister. 'Don't you dare go animal on me! I'm not letting you ruin this bandage. And there's no point going any further with you stumbling like this.'

She wouldn't have stumbled if they'd given her the sword-stick. But the soft grass beyond the muddy bank felt too good for her to argue as her triplets jointly pushed her down. The ground wrapped around her in a warm, comforting embrace, and her eyes fell closed with pure relief. The earth hummed contentedly beneath her head. Insects buzzed busily above her, while the stream splashed a steady lulling tune nearby.

For the first time in her life, she fell into sleep on the unshielded ground in her own original form, with no thick stone floors between her body and the earth and no animal transformation to disguise her true self.

Her last defences slipped silently away … and a new set of voices began to whisper in her head.

8

Shhhhh, a hundred voices seemed to murmur as she drifted, unsure if she was dreaming or awake. *Shhhhh, young one. We have you, now, after all our years of waiting. We will heal you.*

You are ours and always have been.

It was too much for her tired brain to untangle. Letting out a long, defeated sigh, Cordelia fell the rest of the way into deep sleep, cradled by the rustling green forest. In her dreams, the hundred voices kept on whispering to each other, but this time they were too low for her to make out any words. A giant heartbeat drummed deep in the soil underneath her, keeping perfect time with her own. Green grew up through her body, spreading rich, vibrant tendrils along her limbs. Birds kept watch in the trees, guarding her rest, while insect sentries buzzed through the air.

She was loved. She was safe. She was part of a whole. She was …

She woke with a sudden jerk of warning. The insects' hum had halted.

Her eyes snapped open. 'Something's coming,' she said with flat certainty.

Rosalind had been pacing a silent perimeter around the space where Cordelia slept, while Giles sat nearby, his fingers tapping a pattern in mid-air as if he were strumming an invisible lute. His hand stilled as he repeated blankly, '*Something?*'

'The forest isn't happy.' Cordelia wasn't even thinking about her words; she was straining with all her senses for clues as she pushed herself up to a sitting position. Her side ached when she moved, but not as much as it had earlier. The pain was much better. *Surprisingly* better.

But Giles sounded even more alarmed than before. '*The forest isn't happy?*' he repeated. 'What's *that* supposed to mean?'

'Your magic,' Cordelia said impatiently. 'Is it still going, drawing those knights away from us?'

'Ah … no. It ran out, actually. A while back.' His shoulders hunched. 'Well, that's the problem with not training, I guess. I can't keep it under control for very long. But they were running in the opposite direction, so—'

'I can't hear anyone.' Rosalind had found herself a new and thicker stick while Cordelia was sleeping. She held it like a club as she drew closer to the other two, standing between them and the nearest trees.

'The animals can. They're hiding.' The world had rebalanced itself around Cordelia while she'd slept; the ground stayed perfectly steady beneath her feet this time as she stood, without any need for a stick's support. She rubbed hard with one foot at the bent grass where she'd lain, trying to hide the evidence from their hunters.

Then her eyes narrowed.

There hadn't been any flowers growing there before. Now a curving arc of small white starflowers blossomed like a map, outlining exactly where her body had curled.

Goosebumps prickled across her skin as her left hand rose instinctively to touch her waist. Her injury wasn't burning any more. In fact, she could have sworn that it had actually *healed*.

What sort of dream had she just had?

Giles was jittering nervously in place, a distraction in the corner of her vision. 'If those knights are back and heading our way—'

'Can you tell how many of them are coming after us this time?' Rosalind asked Cordelia.

There was *something* tingling at the edge of her hearing, almost like a whisper – more than one? – trying to reach her from far away, but—

'No.' She tore her eyes away from the white flowers and let out her held breath in frustration. 'I just know they'll be here any moment.'

'Then we need to go. *Now.*' Rosalind thrust out her old sword-stick. 'Here. Use this again—'

'No. I don't need it any more.' It felt like a wrench to turn her back on those starflowers. They meant *something*; she was sure of it. But there was no time to explore that mystery now. Cordelia waved off her sister's offer and pointed. 'The forest ends that way. It's our closest path out.'

'Connall really let you explore all the way to the edge of the forest?' Giles frowned.

'Of course he didn't! I just …' I *just know it* was the honest answer, but none of them had ever seen a map of the forest. She *couldn't* know.

And yet …

'Well, it has to end eventually, no matter which way we go,' said Rosalind, 'and that direction leads away from home, so it should take us away from the knights too. Let's do it.'

Squaring her shoulders, she lowered her head like an

angry goat and waved her stick-club threateningly at her siblings. 'Go!'

They went. Cordelia's side didn't even twinge as she launched herself forward. The ripped sides of her gown flew out around her as she ran. Giles's legs were the longest by far and the fastest too, but he slowed more and more after the first minute, staring at her instead of at the trees and brambles that blocked their way.

'Why aren't you bleeding through your bandage?' he demanded. 'How are you even—?'

'*Run!*' Rosalind snarled at both of them.

The whole forest was urging them on now. Cordelia could feel the air thickening behind her, trying to press her further from the danger. A sudden cacophony of angry birdcalls sounded behind them.

'They've reached the stream,' Cordelia panted to her triplets.

'*How do you know?*' Giles's whisper sounded like a shriek as he leaped over a fallen tree trunk, gangly legs flashing in mid-air.

'Faster!' gritted Rosalind.

Up ahead, bright golden light lanced through the canopy of leaves, painting long, vivid stripes along the ivy-covered tree trunks. There was more space between those trees ahead; more room for light to fall. The air tasted different too: like distant smoke and strange, enticing new scents.

They were nearing the end of the forest. They had to be.

Not far behind them, something crashed.

'You two, keep going.' Rosalind skidded to a halt and swerved around, brandishing her stick-club. 'I'll slow them down.'

'No!' Giles staggered, eyes wild and long legs tangling as he spun around mid-leap. 'Mother said to stay together, remember? We're family!'

'I'm *defending* the family,' Rosalind growled, 'and this time, *no one* is stopping me. Go!'

There was no use talking to Rosalind when she was in a battering-ram mood. Cordelia didn't even try. She just lunged forward and *grabbed*, ready to change shape in an instant if she needed to force her stubborn sister forward.

Before her hand could land on Rosalind's arm, though, a sudden trill of music lanced through her.

It wasn't coming from the air. It was a flute piping directly through her veins – high, eerie, and hauntingly familiar. As if—

'Mother!' Cordelia grabbed both of her triplets at once. 'She's here. Run!' She swerved to the left, tugging them with her. For once, they didn't even try to resist.

'What are you talking about?' Giles panted.

'She's here?' Rosalind's head swivelled as she ran. 'Where—?'

'It's her song!' *That* was how Cordelia had recognised the melody. How many times had it rocked them to sleep when they were little? It was the same song Alys had hummed in the garden only yesterday – but Alys couldn't send songs by magic. Only Mother could.

'I don't hear anything,' Rosalind said.

'Just trust me!' Those other messages had streamed through the trees and the earth, as if the forest itself were whispering through her skin, but this song was different. It came through her bones with a magic that felt inescapably familiar. She *knew* it every bit as firmly as she knew that their hunters were nearly upon them now.

'Wait.' Giles was panting for breath. 'I can hear it now too. Cordy's right. It's—'

'*Our lullaby!*' Rosalind finished on a sudden gasp – and sped up to run by Cordelia's side, no longer waiting for directions.

Another five feet, over the brink of a large, grassy clearing, and—

Snap! The air closed behind them.

Rosalind whirled around, raising her stick-club. 'What was that?'

'We're safe.' Cordelia slumped to a halt, breathing hard. 'Can't you feel it?' A blurry, translucent wall of air had formed at the edge of the large clearing, closing them in. 'We're shut off from all the rest of the forest now.'

Giles poked one finger at the shimmering air, eyes wide. 'I can't break through this.'

'Neither can they.' She hoped not, anyway.

Six bear-knights hurtled into the trees they'd just run through, followed by a thin, panting man in a strange crimson robe. Cordelia braced to find out if she'd been right.

Their blurred heads turned, visibly searching. Their voices were muffled by the wall of air. The man in the crimson robe shook his head, his gaze skating past the triplets without a single pause. One of the knights scowled and slashed an arm furiously through the air.

All six knights and their companion turned in unison ... and ran in the opposite direction.

'You see?' A warm, confident voice spoke just behind the three children. 'You're perfectly safe now, my dears.'

That wasn't Mother's voice.

Every sense prickled with warning as Cordelia turned.

In the centre of the clearing, where she'd seen nothing but green grass before, a small white cottage rose up before them. Ivy climbed up its plastered sides; wide, dark timbers framed the open door.

Standing in that doorway, a tall dark-haired woman smiled out at them.

She had Mother's eyes and her hawk-like nose. But silver threaded through her hair, which was perfectly smooth and sleek, not wild and curling like Mother's. It wasn't even trying to burst free from the beaded net that held it back.

Giles gulped audibly. 'You – what—?'

'Oh, *really*.' Tsking disapprovingly, she took a gliding step forward, like a swan crossing water. 'You poor children. Hasn't your mother told you anything about me?'

'We thought *you* were Mother,' Cordelia said hoarsely. 'That song – the one you sent us—'

'That was always her favourite lullaby, wasn't it?' The woman's full lips curved wider. 'She sang it to Connall so often, I knew you'd recognise it too.'

'But … how?' Rosalind's stick-club sagged along with her shoulders, her whisper a bare thread of sound.

'Isn't it obvious? I've been waiting for years.' Her voice was rich with satisfaction as she looked from one to the other in turn. 'Finally – *finally!* – I've been allowed to meet my youngest grandchildren.'

9

Giles led the way to the cottage while a stunned-looking Rosalind took rearguard. She left her stick-club abandoned on the ground, but she shook her head again and again in tight wordless jerks, her harsh breaths snorting against Cordelia's unbound hair.

Cordelia could hear chickens clucking somewhere nearby, but she couldn't see any of them. All that she could see past their grandmother's commanding figure was those bright white cottage walls latticed by nearly black beams in a pattern that looked horribly like bars on a grate ... A grate that was about to close all three of them inside.

She couldn't have spoken even if she'd wanted to.

As always, Giles more than made up for his sisters' silence. 'Are you *really* our grandmother? Well, of course you must be. Look at you!' Half laughing, he ran one hand through his thick red hair until it stood up like the feathers of a startled chick. 'But why didn't Mother ever tell us about you? And why didn't you come with her and Alys and Connall into the forest in the first place? If—'

'Shh.' She shook her head, an indulgent look in her dark eyes. 'You'll have answers to all your questions soon enough. But you children have been lost and alone and afraid, haven't you? You'll want food and drink before anything else.'

'Cordelia's been hurt.' Rosalind spoke abruptly, coming out of her daze. 'She has a wound that needs treating.'

Cordelia shook her head sharply – it didn't need treating, not any more, and she didn't want to talk about that *at all* – but it was too late. Their grandmother's head tilted, eyes sharpening. 'Are you hurt, my dear? I *thought* that stain on your gown looked like blood. Shall I look at it now? Or would you prefer a bite of breakfast first?'

Cordelia had to force her lips to relax enough to speak. 'Breakfast,' she said tightly. 'Nothing else.'

Giles's eyebrows soared at her tone; she ignored him.

Alys had taught them all better manners than that. But Cordelia's muscles were braced to run, and she couldn't loosen them no matter how she tried. Of course they were safe here. Anyone who looked twice at their grandmother would *know* she must be family. Yet it took

73

all Cordelia's strength to keep herself standing at the edge of the waiting cottage instead of fleeing outright for the freedom of the forest.

She felt as wild and irrational as the feral beast her triplets sometimes called her. But no matter how senseless it seemed even to her, she wasn't letting *anyone* look at her definitely healed wound … especially not their newly discovered grandmother.

'Breakfast would be wonderful,' said Giles loudly. 'We're all hungry, aren't we, Ros?'

'Starving,' Rosalind agreed. Her shoulders relaxed, and she stepped to Cordelia's side, smiling at last. 'Thank you, Gra—I mean—'

'Oh, it's perfectly all right to call me Grandmother for now.' Their grandmother nodded graciously and turned to lead the way into the house. Her voice floated back to them over the shoulder of her faded green gown, which showed the signs of multiple mendings. 'Of course, if we were at court in front of onlookers, you'd have to address me as "Your Ladyship" or "Lady Elianora", but—'

'At court!' Giles pulled away from his sisters to hurry after her. 'Do you usually live at the royal court?'

'Not … for some time. But here – see for yourself.' She stepped aside, gesturing at the single open room that filled the cottage. 'My humble abode.'

It might have been small, but it didn't look humble to Cordelia's eyes, not compared to the plain stone rooms of their own home. This one *glittered*, from the sparkling embroidered tapestries that covered the plastered walls and hung from the wooden rafters above their heads, to the heavy-looking golden goblet that sat on the table in the centre of the room. A polished cedar chest hulked in the far corner, so big that Cordelia could have curled up inside it with plenty of room to spare. Several glinting silver bracelets lay arranged in a wide arc across its lid.

'Is that real gold?' Wide-eyed, Giles pointed at the goblet.

'Oh, you poor child. You've never even seen real gold before?' Grandmother *tsk*d again. 'Your mother! Well, we've had our disagreements, of course, but those are long in the past. This is a moment for celebration. Come, sit.' She waved them to the small, oddly shaped table. 'Tell me all about yourselves! This is my first chance to know my own grandchildren. I can already tell that you'll be full of surprises.'

Every animal sense in Cordelia's body screamed for her to back away. But Giles was already loping across the rush-covered floor, and Rosalind took her own place at the table half a minute later, rubbing her hands and looking eagerly towards the big black pot that simmered on the fireplace, sending sweet tendrils of scent throughout the room.

'Come on, Cordy!' she said. 'What are you waiting for?'

Cordelia had no reasonable human answer … and she *wasn't* a mindless animal, no matter what anyone else said. So she lifted one foot and then the other, gritting her teeth with effort, until she stood in their grandmother's cottage and the door fell closed behind her, shutting out the green forest and the world beyond.

Her vision blurred with panic. Her breath shortened.

'There, now. We can make ourselves comfortable.' Their grandmother's voice curled around her, tugging her gently across the room. Cordelia barely even felt her legs move. Her vision only began to clear again as she sat down at the table. It must have been the base of an enormous oak tree, once. It had been polished to an astonishing sheen, just like the golden goblet at its centre.

'You must be thirsty.' Grandmother was suddenly just behind her; the wide, draping silk sleeve of her gown brushed against Cordelia's shoulder as she poured a sweet-smelling liquid into the big goblet. Steam rose from its golden lips. 'Why don't the three of you share this while I prepare your porridge?'

The drink that she'd poured smelt like summer sunshine in a goblet. It smelt like comfort, drawing all of them close together. In fact …

Tears burned at the back of Cordelia's eyes at the scent-memory. It smelt just like the herbs that Mother gathered to increase her own protective magic back at home. And Grandmother had been right – Cordelia *was* thirsty, desperately so, although she hadn't noticed it before. She'd been too busy running through the forest, following the call of family.

Family!

'Mother needs your help.' Her voice was hoarse; she had to yank herself away from that enticing smell as Giles and Rosalind tussled over who would take the first sip from the big, heavy goblet. 'Those knights who were chasing us – they're with the Dukes of Lune and Arden. They're all keeping her prisoner, and they've got Connall and Alys too. They were trying to catch us, but—'

'You needn't worry about them.' Grandmother's long, slender fingers brushed gently against her shoulder. 'No one outside can even see this cottage. Remember? I've been preparing for this moment for twelve long years. I haven't left any room for accidents.'

Cordelia blinked, trying to focus through the distractions beside her. Rosalind had won the battle with Giles and was gulping down liquid from the goblet in long, luxuriant swigs that sent waves of delicious scent washing through the air. Cordelia swallowed over her parched throat and forced herself to keep her eyes on their grandmother. 'So you knew—'

'That they'd eventually break through all Kathryn's spells? Of course. I devoted years of my life to your mother's training. I know her magical limits as well as I know my own.' With an indulgent smile, Grandmother put one hand out to stop Rosalind from taking another sip. 'Do leave enough for the others, dear.'

'Sorry, Grandmother. It just tastes so good!' Rosalind gave her a happy smile, looking as sublimely relaxed as if they were home already, with everything sorted and back to normal. Her voice slurred into a yawn as she finished, 'It's *so* good to be with family again and finally know the right thing—ohh!' Her strong fingers slipped on the goblet's stem. She blinked in surprise at her own misbehaving hand, and Giles grabbed the drink just in time.

'*You* need more sleep, ninny.' Tipping his head back, he took a long sip and closed his eyes in appreciation. '*Mmmm!*'

A low whimper of envy escaped Cordelia's throat; she cringed at the sound, but Grandmother chuckled.

'Don't worry,' she said. 'He'll leave enough for you. Won't you, dear?'

Giles didn't answer. He was too busy gulping down even more, his face slack with bliss. Next to Cordelia, Rosalind had slumped in her seat, abandoning her usual stiff-backed knightly posture to rest her chin on her fist and let her eyes fall closed; she looked as if she could happily forget everything else and snore all day now that the three of them were finally safe again.

But safety had never been enough for Cordelia. She needed freedom, and for that, she needed *answers*.

'Why *didn't* you move into the forest with Mother and the others?' she asked their grandmother. 'And why is it so dangerous for anyone to sit on the Raven Throne? And—'

'My goodness!' Grandmother shook her head ruefully, rattling the black beads in her hairnet. 'You're as full of awkward questions as your mother, aren't you?'

'*Mother?*' Cordelia's brows shot upward in disbelief. 'She won't even *listen* to any questions!'

'Well, I shall,' said Grandmother, 'but first –' she slid the goblet out of Giles's fingers and, reluctantly, he let it go – 'have a drink, dear girl, before you do any more talking. Your throat is terribly dry, isn't it? This will make everything so much easier, I promise.'

It was impossible to argue. The goblet settled in Cordelia's hands with the solid weight of comfort.

Delicious steam rose to fill her senses, and she closed her eyes to savour the sensation.

Then she snapped them back open, forcing herself to lower the goblet before she could take a single sip. 'We have to talk about Mother first,' she said, '*and* Connall and Alys and how we can get them all free from those horrible dukes. They need us! If we don't—'

'Your mother,' said Grandmother, 'made her own decisions long ago without a thought to the consequences for anyone else. *Now.*' Her voice hardened, and her long fingers closed around Cordelia's smaller hand, raising the goblet firmly to Cordelia's chin. '*Drink!*'

Cordelia's lips parted in surprise. Obediently, she tilted the cup under the pressure of Grandmother's strong fingers. The first taste met her tongue in a splash of delight.

A loud *thump!* beside her made her lower the goblet with a start. Rosalind's chin had slid off her fist and sent her toppling forehead-first on to the oak table. Even that impact hadn't woken her, though. She sprawled out, snoring, with her arms and legs outflung at angles that looked horribly painful.

'Silly,' mumbled Giles on Rosalind's other side. 'Making all that noise!' His eyes had only half opened at the sound; he closed them again now as he slid further and further down, until he'd curled his long limbs comfortably across the round table, resting his head on their sister's prone body. 'Jus' lie down for a nap, that's all, no fuss or performance ...' His voice trailed off into a drifting snore.

'Poor dears,' Grandmother murmured gently. 'You're *so* tired from your adventures all alone in the forest. But you can rest now. You're with family again.'

Family. That much was true.

But Cordelia's head was spinning with the steam from her drink, and the images before her warped and melded into senseless combinations against her will. Giles and Rosalind both spread out before her, loose-limbed and vulnerable. Their grandmother, with their mother's familiar eyes and nose, smiled victoriously down at them ...

... Grandmother, who had waited twelve years for this moment, and whom no one else in the family had ever mentioned.

Dread crawled on spider legs through Cordelia's stomach. Her voice came out as a whisper as she rose from her seat, setting the goblet back on to the table. 'What *were* you waiting to do, all these years?' she demanded. 'And why would my drinking this make everything easier?'

'Oh, dear. And here I thought you might be the clever one!' Sighing, Grandmother put one hand on Cordelia's shoulder and pushed her back down into place. 'Isn't it obvious? Drinking this will make everything easier for *me*, because it'll stop you from trying to escape! My daughter caused me so much trouble over the years with her attempts. But do you know what, my dear?'

Grabbing Cordelia's chin in her free hand, she leaned even closer, until her hawk nose bumped against her granddaughter's, and her familiar/unfamiliar face filled Cordelia's vision like a waking nightmare. 'I've had twelve years to learn from my mistakes,' she murmured. 'This time, I won't allow *any* accidents to happen. So I *will* be the one to hand you, personally, to the Dukes of Arden and Lune tomorrow, to win back all the wealth and power that your mother stole from me for your sakes – and *no one*, especially not my own grandchildren, will stop me!'

Cordelia's head was still spinning, but that couldn't stop her now. She lunged forward, screaming with all her might—

But Grandmother was too strong. Grabbing Cordelia's nose with one hand, she pinched it tightly shut. Long fingernails jabbed into Cordelia's skin. Then she lifted the steaming goblet to Cordelia's mouth and *pushed*.

Cordelia's screams were full of bubbles. She couldn't even focus enough to shift shapes. Everything turned into a desperate, wordless blur as she twisted and struggled in her grandmother's iron grip. Sweet liquid gushed down her throat no matter how hard she gagged and tried to spit it out.

The last thing she heard, as sleep closed smothering arms around her, was her grandmother's sigh of perfect satisfaction.

10

'Cordelia. *Cordelia!*'

Still deep in sleep, she whimpered with frustration. Would her bothersome family *never* leave her alone? Connall wouldn't stop shouting no matter how hard she tried to stay wrapped in blissful dreams of dappled leaves and rippling streams.

Didn't he understand that she was tired?

'*Cordelia!*'

'What?' she finally snarled – and woke with a gasp at the eerie, echoing sound of her own voice. Her back hit a cold stone wall, hard.

Her eyes shot open.

She sat in a tiny room that she'd never seen before. It was as round as a kitchen well, lit by dim streaks of sunlight, and barely two paces wide. A latticed grate covered the single high window, its bars criss-crossing like the dark latticed beams that had covered Grandmother's white cottage …

What had happened to Grandmother's cottage?

Where *was* she?

'Finally.' Connall's big hands closed around her shoulders and gripped hard. He let out a shuddering breath.

She yanked her gaze away from the barred window and finally took in her older brother's face. Heavy shadows sagged beneath his dark brown eyes, and his thin face looked tight with strain. 'I've been trying to reach you for hours!' He gave her shoulders a gentle shake. 'Where *are* you three hiding, anyway?'

He really didn't know. She could see it in his face.

Nothing about this made any sense.

'Where are *you*?' she demanded. 'Is Alys all right? Where's Mother? And where are we now?' Pulling free, she turned in place on the bare stone flooring and stretched out her arms to brush the ends of her fingertips against both curving sides of the miniature room. Cold seeped through the rough stone walls and down her arms – not quite as solid as reality, but far more true than any natural dream. 'Is this where you're being kept prisoner?'

He shook his head. 'This room is a memory of mine from before you were born. The place I'm being kept this time is … different.' His voice tightened. 'Alys was healed. I saw that much, but I haven't seen her since. I don't know where Mother is, either. She can't touch her magic, so I can't reach out to her. I was lucky they only had one collar prepared, so they couldn't trap my magic the way they trapped hers – but I've only just gathered enough of my strength back to try reaching the three of you.'

He shook his head, looking infinitely weary. 'I don't know why I thought back to this room when I cast the vision to bring all of us together – it's where I was kept long before you were born – but—'

'Wait.' She stared up at him. 'You were kept a prisoner in this room *before* I *was born*? But you were only little, then!' Her brows bunched together. 'Does this have something to do with Grandmother?'

Connall gaped down at her, fingers loosening from her shoulders. 'What do you know about our grandmother?'

She narrowed her eyes at him. 'If anyone had ever bothered to answer *my* questions—'

'Please,' her older brother whispered, 'tell me you haven't actually met her. Tell me she doesn't have you three in her grasp now.'

Cordelia didn't answer.

A sickly-sweet fog was wrapped around her most recent memories. What *had* happened just before she'd come here? She'd been asleep – she knew that much. And she had been at Grandmother's house before that. She remembered stepping inside that white-and-black cottage. She remembered sweet steam clouding everything, blurring her thoughts and turning into a thick fog of sleep.

Sweet steam, choking liquid, and Grandmother's eyes, dark and predatory and triumphant …

'What's wrong?' Connall asked sharply. 'Why are you shaking?'

Shivers rippled convulsively through her body. She wrapped her arms around herself, trying to hold them in. 'There was something in the drink she gave all of us. It made us fall asleep. I tried not to drink any of it after I saw the others, but she – she—'

'She forced you,' Connall finished grimly. 'Of course she did. Lady Elianora *never* lets her family deny her will. That's why she took me prisoner last time. Mother tried to say no to getting married a second time.' His lips twisted. 'And *that's* why you were the only one I could reach with my summoning now. *You* struggled, so her potion didn't take you under completely. The others trusted her, so they never had a chance.'

'But she's family!' The words tore out of Cordelia's mouth like a cry of pain. 'We were supposed to be safe once we found her!'

'Those dukes are family too. Hadn't you realised?' Connall took a step back, running a trembling hand over his hair. 'Your *father* was a first cousin to both of them. Every high family in this kingdom has mixed and tangled over the years – but all *we* are to any of them is pawns in the game they've been playing for decades, ever since the Raven Crown first cracked.'

'*Cracked?*' Cordelia frowned up at him. 'What do you mean? There are still kings and queens, so—'

'The *original* Raven Crown is what started this whole nightmare in the first place.' Connall groaned, turning away and rattling off the words like a lesson that he'd learned by heart long ago. 'It was created with old magics at the first founding of the kingdom, and it bound the ruler and the land together for everybody's sake. It stayed that way for centuries of peace. But thirty years ago, it cracked and fell off King Kalmen's head because he'd broken the old contracts with the land beyond repair.

'Of course, every high family in the land said that *they* should be the ones to rule after Kalmen's failure … and since then, the fighting has never stopped, because without that original crown, there's no magical proof to seal any choice for good. Not one heir has ever managed to wear it, no matter how many sorcerers tried to mend it with their spells.

'By now, no one's even trying to fix it any more. They just buried the broken pieces at Raven's Nest, high in the mountains where the oldest spirits of the land are still hiding and holding all our deepest secrets safe. Everyone's given up on those founding magics nowadays. The six great houses – Arden, Lune, Harcourt, Solenne, Breville and Mordaunt – only care about the wealth and the power of the throne. They don't mind who gets hurt along the way.'

'So we can't even trust our own family?' Cold was seeping all through Cordelia's body now. White mist curled at the corners of her vision, obscuring the grey stone walls. Her nose twitched as an unfamiliar smell drifted past, distracting and unsettling.

'Trust *me*,' said her older brother fiercely. 'Trust Mother, trust Alys, and thank all the surviving spirits of the land that you and Giles and Rosalind are still together. But you have to understand ...'

He let out a long breath. 'Mother would *never* have fled into the forest if she could have helped it. You know how she hates to back down from any fight – but she knew she couldn't protect any of us if she stayed. First *my* father was killed in one of these stupid, endless battles over the crown, and then Lady Elianora took me hostage to force Mother into marrying again.'

He took a shuddering breath, then shook his head hard. 'Mother got me back, though, when she agreed to remarry for the family's sake. And your father – oh, Cordy, if you'd only known him! Grandmother might have chosen him for his position, but the way he loved Mother *and* loved me – we both ended up loving him too. How could we not? He said he was my father, no matter how we'd come together. He made family feel *safe*. But then he died fighting for a different heir. No one can ever hang on to that throne without the Raven Crown to seal it!

'Mother swore she wouldn't let any of her children be stolen from her ever again, by her mother or by the throne – but everyone knew by then that she was pregnant. None of our families would *ever* let any heirs out of their grasp. I may not remember much from that time, but …'

His face twisted as he glanced at the cold stone walls that curved around them. 'I remember *enough* – and I swore, even then, that Lady Elianora would never get hold of me again. I would have done anything to stay safe from her and keep you all safe too.' His hands fisted at his sides. 'We *had* to get out, no matter what it took.'

'But why didn't Mother just explain all that to us?' Cordelia demanded. 'If she'd only—ahh!'

White mist was suddenly curling up her legs, thick and sticky and cold, stretching tingling, grasping fingers towards her hands and arms to pull her down within it. Lurching away, she kicked out desperately – but that only made the mist cling even more closely to her gown and her shoes. The rough stone walls of Connall's vision should have pressed firmly against her back, but all she felt now was a damp and spongy sensation, like cloudbanks rising to suck her in.

'We're running out of time.' Connall's jaw clenched. This time, when he reached out for her, she couldn't feel his fingers against her skin. They passed through her like ghosts. 'The sorcerers here must have felt what I'm doing. They're already trying their best to break my casting. They'll be here any moment now.'

'What will they do to you?' Cordelia demanded.

'Don't worry about that. Just … I tried *so hard* to protect you all these years! That's why I listened to Mother and kept those secrets from you. I just wanted you three to grow up feeling safe! I never wanted you to be afraid. Not like …' His face twisted in anguish as he glanced around the fading prison cell. 'Just get free of Lady Elianora. No matter what it takes!'

'But how?' Cordelia demanded. 'Mother didn't give any of *us* magic lessons. We don't know how to—'

'You all have your own powers.' His voice was growing faint, but the desperation in his tone rang through. 'Remember Alys's river stone! Every spell can be broken if you find the right key. You just have to get out – and then *run*, as fast and as far as you can! Don't turn back for anything. Just *go*.'

Thumps sounded in the distance, beyond the wavering stone walls. Panic flashed across his face. His lean brown cheeks hollowed.

'We're going to rescue you,' Cordelia promised her older brother. 'Don't worry. You won't be a prisoner for long. We'll come back for all of you.'

'No! Don't you dare, Cordeli—*ahh!*'

White mist billowed through the stone room like a snowstorm …

… And Cordelia plunged awake – truly awake, this time – gulping deep, harsh breaths that nearly burst open her chest as the echoes of her older brother's panicked shout rang in her ears.

Utter blackness surrounded her. Connall was gone.

Stale air tickled against her nose and mouth. There wasn't nearly enough of it. Something heavy lay on top of her, crushing her chest and legs and pushing down into her face until it nearly smothered her. Itchy fabric brushed against her cheeks and forehead. Something hard and painful pushed into her lower back. *Why couldn't she see?*

All she could smell was sweat and grime and …

Cedar!

Cordelia shoved and squirmed, panting with effort. Her chest burned. Her muscles screamed with discomfort. Finally, she managed to wriggle one arm free to reach out through the unrelenting blackness.

She touched wood scant inches from her face.

Now she knew exactly where she was.

Grandmother must have piled her, Giles and Rosalind into that massive cedar chest and left them there, all packed neatly in place to be delivered to the dukes. That was one of Giles's knobbly elbows bruising her lower back right now, while Rosalind's own strong back pressed down against Cordelia's face … and neither of them had so much as shifted in place no matter how roughly she'd struggled in these last few minutes.

The spell still held both of them fully in its grip … and Cordelia was squashed between them. *Trapped.*

Or at least, that must be what Grandmother thought.

Cordelia's upper lip lifted in a wolfish snarl.

Lady Elianora should have taken the time to learn more about her younger grandchildren as people, not just as pawns in her own plans … because Cordelia's fear washed away under a tidal wave of fury as she lay crushed in the pitch darkness between her triplets.

This time, there was no sweet-smelling spell-steam to confuse her. This time, she could focus ... and she had sworn never to allow herself to be trapped again.

A moment later, Rosalind landed on Giles with a soft *thump* as Cordelia's human body vanished from between them. A tiny black beetle scuttled on six swift legs up the flat sides of the chest. It slid swiftly out through the keyhole, squeezing easily past the big old key that sat so smugly in the lock.

Cordelia was free and uncaged once more ... and Grandmother was about to discover just how troublesome her long-lost grandchildren could be.

11

From her perch on top of the locked cedar chest, Cordelia looked around Grandmother's cottage with multifaceted beetle eyes and saw a dozen different views at once, arranged into a dazzling puzzle before her. Every different shape loomed overwhelmingly high; all the angles were off balance, and Grandmother was nowhere to be seen. Was she even in the cottage any longer?

Cordelia reached out with two thin, secretive antennae and tasted the air, testing it for information.

She couldn't hear anything in beetle form, but she felt the vibrations like a drumbeat. Grandmother was definitely here and moving around the floor.

If she'd been the one to train Mother in magic, she could turn Cordelia human again in a heartbeat.

Shifting forms, Cordelia fluttered up into the dusty rafters high above the room to listen and wait for the perfect moment. A dull grey moth wouldn't be noticed hiding among all these cobwebbed beams above the dangling tapestries – and moths, unlike beetles, had brilliant hearing. Picking a dark corner to perch in, she wafted her sensitive wings to catch every scrap of sound that floated up to her from below.

Grandmother was humming to herself. It wasn't the family lullaby this time; it was a tune that Cordelia had never heard before, lilting and flicking like steps in a dance, and Grandmother sashayed across the floor as she hummed it. 'Almost … almost there … Oh, my goodness, it's the famous Lord Haldemere, isn't it?'

She laughed, a low, delighted sound, and flicked out a cloth as she spun around, dropping into a mock curtsey for her imaginary audience. 'Why, yes, it *has* been some time since you've seen me at court, my lord. But what a pity for *you* that I've returned, because I happen to have an excellent memory! I remember *all* your plots against me. And as grandmother to the new ruler and greatly favoured by their regents – well! Who knows just what I might choose to do? Perhaps I'll let you wonder and wait for a time before I decide upon my perfect revenge. Or perhaps, if I'm feeling *really* generous …'

Fully absorbed in her grandmother's words and movements, Cordelia hadn't even realised that she was moving, herself – until she found herself fluttering half an inch below the furthest rafter, well on her way back into full view. The light from the flames in the fireplace had drawn her without a conscious thought. *Stupid moths!*

She flapped swiftly back upward, every sense still attuned to her grandmother's vicious stream of words.

'You don't think much of my grandchild, my lord? Well, neither do I, to be perfectly frank. But everyone knows that a child-ruler is ruled by their regents, and when their regents can be persuaded – or enspelled – into good sense ... well, then, what *can't* we do with them, eh?'

The receptors in Cordelia's wings took in every word, storing them all up to dissect and stew over later.

And then the tip of her right wing touched something sticky. Startled, she twisted in mid-air to yank her wing free ... and the glistening, waiting spiderweb captured her left wing too.

Grandmother was still practising her greetings down below, but high up in the rafters, panic flooded Cordelia's fragile body. Frantically, she wriggled and twisted to get free. Every turn only tangled her deeper and deeper within the web. Pictured again and again in her fractured view, a giant spider raced across the glimmering strands towards her on a rippling wave of giant, hairy brown legs.

To a human, that spider might have been hand-sized. From Cordelia's perspective, it was overwhelming.

Her tiny moth-body was frantic to escape, and panic gave those instincts full control. No matter how hard she tried, Cordelia couldn't stop the useless thrashing of her wings. But she was still a girl inside, and she knew the truth: no moth could possibly escape from this.

Even if she turned herself into a spider, tangled as she was now, she might still be prey to the web's guardian. But if she changed into anything strong enough to break free, how could Grandmother *not* notice what was happening right above her?

Cordelia's wings whirred frantically within their trap. The spider's hairy brown body settled into place just above her, filling every facet of her compound vision. Its jointed jaw cracked open. Dark fangs flashed. Venom trembled at their tips …

And the web broke with a **snap** as Cordelia lunged upward. Her tiny, helpless moth-body had shifted into a massive black crow, whose claws ripped the web around her to hapless shreds. Her long, sharp beak seized the big brown spider and swallowed it whole with a harsh '*Cawwww!*' of defiance.

Grandmother's voice cut off abruptly below.

Too late to be stealthy now! Cordelia tore her way free of the web-dense rafters and dived down like vengeance with her long claws fiercely outstretched.

Some things are instinctive even for the most powerful people. Faced with a screaming crow diving directly at her eyes, Grandmother flinched, hands flying up to shield her face. It was only for an instant – but that was enough. Cordelia swooped over her dark head and through the high, narrow window beyond, where the wooden shutter had been propped open to let bright daylight inside.

Black feathers scattered in her wake as she squeezed through. Only a moment later, she was a tiny, near-invisible mosquito hovering against the outer wall above the window – and as the front door of the cottage burst open and Grandmother lunged outside in pursuit, she nipped swiftly and silently back in.

'*Run!*' Connall had ordered her. '*Don't turn back for anything!*' But she wasn't running anywhere without Giles and Rosalind. Families were *supposed* to protect each other, even if her own grandmother didn't understand that.

Turning back into girl form, she lunged across the room to wrap her arms around the big, round oak table and half shove, half haul it across the rush-covered floor.

Groaning with effort, she pushed it hard against the door. *There.* With luck, Grandmother would take ages to hunt for the bird who'd so mysteriously attacked her and then disappeared. Anyone trained in magic would have to know there had been nothing natural in *that* attack. She might even think that the bird had been a spy from some rival sorcerer.

But the moment she gave up her search …

Cordelia hurtled across the rushes and dropped to her knees before the cedar chest in the corner, nerves jangling through every breath. With shaking fingers, she turned the heavy copper key and flung open the lid.

'Wake up!' she whisper-screamed at her triplets, who still slept tangled in their pile. '*Wake up now!*'

But they didn't listen to her when they were asleep any more than they did when awake.

Behind her, the door of the cottage rattled. A moan of protest broke from her lips.

Too soon! She hadn't managed to wake either of them yet. She *couldn't* break the spell on her own, no matter what Connall thought. Grandmother's potion was too powerful.

But maybe there was something else that she could do.

Cordelia's gaze settled on the cooling black pot that sat beside the fireplace – and the golden goblet that had fallen in her scramble to push the oak table to the door.

'*What* a clever child you are, my dear!' Grandmother carolled through the door. 'You should have slept for hours yet – but it won't make any difference, you know. Whatever little tricks you're planning – and casting a bird illusion to distract me *was* impressive! – my magic *will* win in the end. Did your mother even bother to train you properly? Or did she keep her own tricks secret, like everything else she hid from you?'

Gritting her teeth, Cordelia scooped up the empty goblet from the floor and started towards the pot.

'How many secrets *have* you ever managed to winkle out of her?' Grandmother crooned. 'It was *so* convenient for Kathryn, wasn't it, to keep you locked up in the forest for all these years? Utterly safe from interference, with no one who'd ever dare let you know the dangerous truth about yourselves … Did she never drop any hints about who you truly are? Or those other brats either?'

Brats?

No one was allowed to insult her triplets. 'You don't know anything about me or my family,' Cordelia snarled. 'But if you're talking about the Raven Crown—'

'Aha!' Grandmother let out a pealing laugh of delight. 'So it *is* you causing all this trouble, little girl. I had a feeling that it might be! The others aren't even awake yet, are they? But *you* were too wild to stay asleep for long.' She breathed her words through the door. 'It's just you and me, now, dear. Do you truly believe you can stand against my magic?'

No. That answer was as obvious as the open window high above, still offering Cordelia one last chance at escape.

Swallowing hard, she took a slow, unhappy step towards the oak table that blocked the door. She knew what she had to do.

'That's it,' Grandmother murmured. 'Come closer, now. The truth is, my dear, the two of us can work together. I only need the Raven heir, you see.' Her words purred through the air, soft and tingling. 'You can go free if you help me now. You're a feral one, aren't you? You'd never fit in at court, I know. It would be miserable for everyone involved. But I can make quite certain that you'll never be chased by any bothersome knights again.'

Cordelia rolled her eyes in disgust. 'Connall already told me that the dukes and duchesses won't ever let go of any possible heirs.'

'Ah, but I know something you don't about this family.' Grandmother's voice dropped to a whisper. 'It all comes down to the mystery of you three children … and your mother's most *unforgivable* secret.' She gave a low hum of anticipation. 'Don't you want to know why she's been so desperate to keep the truth about your past hidden, even from you?'

Cordelia's breath caught in her throat. All those years she'd spent trapped inside without any explanations …

Two images flashed before her eyes:

Mother sinking to her knees as she sent them away. '*I love you all so much.*'

… And Connall's face when he'd realised exactly where they were now. She had never understood, until today, why he had spent his life so afraid.

'I'm not doing *anything* for you, no matter what you promise me.' Shifting shape, Cordelia snapped out hawk wings and pumped hard, clenching strong claws around her burden. *Too heavy, too heavy …*

She had to get higher.

Grandmother's voice was already chanting outside. Something slammed against the front of the door with a *boom*. Wood shavings splintered and flew into the room. The oak table slid an inch across the floor.

Faster! Pain shot through Cordelia's labouring legs and wings.

Giles and Rosalind snored on peacefully behind her.

Slam!

The oak table skidded across the room.

The door flew wide open. Grandmother stalked inside, arms raised to hurl a spell.

With a desperate screech, Cordelia opened her claws and dropped the refilled golden goblet over her grandmother's dark head.

Liquid splashed everywhere. It soaked Grandmother's elegant, beaded hairnet and flooded her face. It filled her mouth too, as she gurgled with shock, tipping her head back and spinning around to search for the source of the attack.

Cordelia saw realisation dawn in those too-familiar dark eyes as their gazes met and clashed. Grandmother's wet face contorted in fury. Her hands rose like claws, preparing to launch more magic. Cordelia wheeled backwards through the air, crying out. She could never fly away in time …

But her grandmother slid to the floor an instant later, arms falling limply to her sides. '*Stupid* girl!' she moaned. Her shoulders hit the ground with a thud. 'Fighting me for those two brats, when …' Her eyes slipped closed with her yawn. 'You're not even … their real sister!'

A moment later she was asleep, her hairnet pillowed in the rushes, with a fresh line of drool slipping down her wet cheek …

… Leaving Cordelia hovering numbly in mid-air with those final words echoing endlessly through her.

12

It was good to be an animal. Good that her triplets – that *Giles and Rosalind* – were still asleep, not awake and asking unanswerable questions.

Cordelia left them piled in the cedar chest. In bear form, she hauled it out of the cottage, bursting through the doorframe and leaving the entrance in a shambles behind her. She shifted back to a girl only for long enough to put together a harness out of Lady Elianora's belongings so that she could drag the heavy chest behind her.

Even *that* was almost too much thinking to endure. She could hardly stand to wait until everything was safely fastened; until she could finally shift and run, straining every muscle with effort, as fast and as hard as she could away from the cottage.

'Trust me. Trust Mother, trust Alys, and thank all the

surviving spirits of the land that you and Giles and Rosalind are still together.'

Did Connall not know the truth about Cordelia either? Or had he been lying to her all along?

Did he even think of himself as her brother?

Her roar sent birds scattering from all the branches ahead. She tipped her head down and pushed herself faster.

Lady Elianora's wall of air had broken when she'd lost consciousness. Cordelia would have burst through it anyway, in this mood. She *wanted* to crash hard against something. To *break* things. She wanted to fight someone with slashing claws and teeth.

She wanted—

She burst through the tree line, panting. The sight ahead of her made all four paws slam to a halt. The heavy chest landed against her with a *thump*. She sagged to the ground, barely aware of the collision.

The forest had ended. It had actually *ended*! She was looking outside for the first time in her life ... and it looked nothing like she had imagined.

All those books that Mother had read aloud and the ballads that Giles had learned from his books were full of great houses and colourful pageantry – or crowded towns overflowing with adventures. She'd expected to find tall buildings everywhere, flying bright flags and full of people.

What she saw instead was a wasteland.

There were no buildings on the vast plain that stretched before her, only bare brown dirt that spread to rolling, dead-brown hills in the far distance. Long furrows branded the plain like scorch marks. She could make out faded patterns in the dirt where rows of plants might once have grown … but no more. Some disaster had ravaged this place and left nothing alive in its wake.

There was no birdsong in the open, echoing air and no hum of insects to tug her forward. Wildflowers and weeds should have covered the abandoned earth. The forest should have sent forth strong roots to gain new ground.

But her big bear body understood why none of that had happened, because the warning shot up through her paws, the scent and message unmistakable to any animal instinct:

Stay away!

This place smelt overwhelmingly *wrong*. It was broken.

She had nowhere else to go.

Cordelia wanted her fierce, enraging mother so intensely that she would have howled with pain if she'd only had the strength left. She would have given *anything* to close her eyes and find herself back inside the protective walls of their stone castle, with no poisonous whispers or hidden truths ever to be uncovered.

Even when Mother's decisions had been infuriating, Cordelia had always known that she was safe, because Mother was in charge, Mother was all-powerful, and Mother would do *anything* to protect her family.

Mother was a prisoner now, because of Cordelia.

… And Cordelia might not even be her real daughter.

Was that why Mother had always said there was no point in trying to harness Cordelia's powers? What kind of magic *did* Cordelia have, anyway? All four of the children were supposed to have been born with the same magical potential to control the world around them with sorcery … but all Cordelia could ever do was shift her own shape. She'd always been half animal inside anyway.

Why didn't her magic work like Connall's and the others'? She had always taken that difference for granted, just as she'd taken her jostling, noisy family for granted … until now.

Even without any real training, when Giles had really needed it, *he'd* been able to use his natural magic to affect the world around him. Mother had always said that Rosalind could do that too. *Cordelia* was the only one who'd been deemed untrainable … and not only in the way that her magic worked.

She was the only one Mother hadn't trusted to know about that tunnel under the moat – because she was the one who had been half feral from the moment she'd been born. She was the one who'd been constantly tugged beyond the safety of their castle walls by an invisible hook in her chest that never seemed to touch any of the others … as if she'd secretly never belonged inside with them in the first place.

Was *that* why the land was talking to her now and the others couldn't hear it? The thought made a shudder ripple through her massive body.

Every time she'd ever flown away to explore, she had *known* that her family, noisy and loving and aggravating, would be waiting for her when she returned. But now …

'We *wouldn't be here at all if she ever stayed where she was supposed to be.*' That was what Giles had said about her that first night, after they'd all been forced to flee.

He'd been right.

Had he and Rosalind even thought they'd had any choice about forgiving her? *They* still thought she was their sister – the only family they had left.

If they ever found out that she wasn't …

She would lose them right now if she sat *thinking* any longer! Lady Elianora was still too close behind. Those dukes and their knights wouldn't give up hunting for them, either.

So Cordelia lumbered back up on to all four padded paws, groaning with the pain of the effort.

She had been waiting all her life to explore outside the forest. Now she picked up one paw at a time and forced herself on to the rough, scarred and broken earth, aiming for those bare hills in the far distance and pulling the heavy cedar chest behind her.

It was almost three hours later, and early evening, when the bumping of the cedar chest against the ground suddenly changed. It was rocking back and forth behind her now, jerking against the makeshift harness and yanking hard. Muffled voices sounded inside.

Finally. Her triplets were awake.

The bubbling feeling that *that* stirred up inside her felt as much like dread as like relief.

She could still pretend she hadn't noticed—

'Cordelia!' they both yelled at once.

'Grr!' Growling with frustration, Cordelia's furry body tipped to a halt on the dry, cracked ground. She would have stayed in bear form to avoid any awkward questions, but she needed human fingers to unstrap the harness and manage the big key in its lock. She turned it carefully until it clicked—

And they had her.

'Thank goodness!' Rosalind surged upward, flinging open the lid. 'I thought I'd choke in there. Giles's stink—'

'*My* stink?' Giles's red head popped up behind her. '*I'm* not the one who—oh.' He blinked at the vast brown earth around them. 'Where are we? Where's Grandmother?'

'We're not in the forest any more.' Rosalind frowned. 'Did those soldiers reach Grandmother's house after all? Did she send us ahead while she fought them off?'

Cordelia opened her mouth … then shut it again. There was too much. She couldn't possibly sum it all up, and her throat was too parched to talk comfortably anyway.

Rosalind was already clambering out of the chest, stepping carelessly across Giles and ignoring his grunts of protest along the way. 'You could've at least taken the time to wake me first.' She landed on the ground and put her hands to her waist, stretching out her back with a grimace. 'I'm bruised all over from being rattled around in there. Couldn't you have tossed in a pillow or two?'

'You *had* a pillow, Ros.' Still crouching in the crate, Giles cranked his neck from side to side. 'I was the one stuck on the bottom with you bumping across me all the way.'

Rolling her eyes, Cordelia turned away from their

squabble to keep on trudging up the steadily rising brown slope. It wouldn't take much longer to reach the hills themselves; she'd been telling herself that for the last half hour, just like she'd been telling herself for ages that she didn't need a drink. She was on two legs, not four any more, though, and she felt unbalanced by the shift – and by the loss of the harness she had worn. There was nothing tethering her down with the others any more; she could just soar alone into the sky and—

'No!' Strong hands seized her right arm. 'No changing shapes! I can *see* you thinking about it.' Short black hair mussed and cheeks bright red, Rosalind glowered at her ferociously. 'You are *not* flying off and leaving us to work out everything for ourselves. Not this time! Just because we happened to fall asleep doesn't mean *you* get to go all feral and—'

'Oh, no.' Giles stared at her, slack-jawed. '*Please* tell me you didn't go into a panic and sneak us all away from Grandmother without telling her!'

Cordelia clenched her own jaw hard.

'Cordelia!' He clutched his rumpled hair, eyes squeezing shut in agony. 'I *know* you didn't take to her, but you have to use your *brain* sometimes, not just your almighty animal instincts. She's—'

'I *saved* you!' The words burst from between Cordelia's

teeth. 'You didn't just *fall asleep*, you fools. It was a potion that she fed us! And Connall said—'

'Connall was there?' Rosalind's head swivelled around, searching. 'Where—?'

'Connall found me in a vision, and Lady *Elianora* wanted to trade us to the dukes. That was her plan all along! She was going to use us to get back into power – just like she took Connall prisoner, years ago, to get Mother back under her control.' Cordelia wrenched herself free from Rosalind's loosened grip. 'I got us away from her while you slept. *You're welcome.* Now you can both take care of yourselves!' She flung herself into the air in a furious whirl of feathers.

It should have been a satisfyingly dramatic escape – but Giles lunged upward and caught her by one thin bird leg.

She *hated* how tall he'd become!

'Shh,' he said as she screeched at him and flapped her wings in challenge. Ignoring all her struggles, he tucked her against his side, his grip firm and inescapable. She would have to genuinely hurt him to get free … and they both knew she never would.

'Just *shush*, Cordy.' His voice wobbled. 'We didn't understand what had happened. That was all.' The bump in his long neck bobbed as he swallowed above her, his face pale. 'We'll talk it all over properly later on. Right now, though …' He looked back and forth across the long, bleak landscape beneath the gradually darkening grey sky. 'Those dukes are still going to be hunting us … and I suppose Grandmother will be too. Ros? Which way do you think we should go?'

Cordelia stuck her head under her left wing just to spite them. She'd *had* a perfectly good plan already. If they'd only bothered to ask …

'Might as well keep going this way, at least for now.' Rosalind's brisk voice carried through all Cordelia's shielding feathers. 'Until we get over these hills, we won't know what's out there. And we're too obvious here. There's nowhere to hide.'

Well, they weren't wrong about *everything*. Cordelia was too exhausted and thirsty to sort them out anyway.

She'd dragged both of them for hours while they'd slept. It was time to close her eyes and let them take a turn. No longer struggling, she burrowed into Giles's lean side and let sleep wrap dark, enveloping wings around her. It closed her off from all the terrible questions she couldn't bear to ask or answer …

And dropped her into a nightmare not her own.

13

In the forest, Cordelia had slept surrounded by cool green whispers, soothing and healing her in her dreams. Here, all that she could hear in her sleep was endless, anguished screaming.

BROKEN! BROKEN!

This part of the land was in *agony*. Screams battered deafeningly at her ears. Blinding red filled her vision. Red *everywhere*.

Flames had raged across this patch of earth again and again, burning every plant that dared shoot out a green bud.

Endless blood had spilt across the ruined crops. Worse yet, it had been *family* blood that drenched them – cousins killing cousins again and again, poisoning the already-wounded ground.

All the old contracts broken. Betrayed!

No wonder plants wouldn't grow nor animals venture on to this scorched plain. Trapped in the interminable screams of the earth, dream-Cordelia curled in on herself, covering her ears and squeezing her eyes shut. It didn't work. Red bled through everything, turning her hands and eyelids transparent. She couldn't escape the land's pain. It was *everywhere*, shrieking for her to *understand* and *do something.*

BROKEN! BROKEN!

'Ahhh!' She jerked awake, flailing, and tumbled from Giles's grip on to the rock-studded brown slope. She landed hard, in girl form, on all the wrong angles.

'Careful!' Giles stared down at her, shaking out the arm he'd used to carry her bird-body. 'We're safe now, remember? You don't need to panic.' He slid a quick glance down the barren hillside, towards the dark forest far in the distance. 'No one's spotted us yet, as far as we can tell, and we're nearly to the top, so—'

'Made it!' Rosalind shouted the words from fifteen feet ahead. She was standing on the rounded summit above them, hands on her hips, glowing with triumph in the last fading light of evening. 'There are *so many* places to take shelter nearby. Look! We'll be safe here overnight, and then—'

'We can't stop anywhere near here! I *can't*.' Trembling convulsively, Cordelia picked herself up. Her fresh bruises ached with every awkward movement. The land's screams echoed in her ears. Now that she'd heard them in her dream, she couldn't shut them off again. They were battering at her from all sides, almost as loudly as they had in her sleep, stealing her sense of balance ... and trying their best to suck her back under their red veil.

Giles had already started loping up the final slope towards Rosalind, but he paused between them now, frowning down at her. 'What do you mean, you *can't*? It's getting dark. You know we'll have to stop soon.'

Rosalind scowled impatiently down at them both from the top of the hill. 'Are you two coming or not?'

Cordelia closed her eyes, fighting for clarity through the haze of echoed pain and fear and dizzying thirst.

Every fear of her own that she'd left behind in sleep was back again, even stronger than before ... and the land's screams were just one more unbearable sign of separation between her and the only family she had left.

They couldn't hear those screams. If she told them that she could, then they would know she was even more different than they'd realised before. Even more *wrong*.

'*Not even their real sister ...*'

'Cordelia,' Giles said, his voice suddenly much closer. 'What's going on?'

Cordelia hated it when people wouldn't answer simple questions. But she couldn't explain. She'd lost so much already. She *couldn't* risk losing any more. She could barely even think through the screaming of the land.

And there was only one thing that she truly *knew* – one line that she had recognised in the nightmare the land had sent her.

All the old contracts broken …

Connall had called those old contracts *the founding magics*, hadn't he? He'd said something else about the broken crown that was linked inexorably to them:

'*They just buried the broken pieces at Raven's Nest, high in the mountains where the oldest spirits of the land are still hiding and holding all our deepest secrets safe.*'

There was so little she could be certain of any more. They had so many impossibly powerful enemies and so little knowledge on their side.

Raven's Nest, she thought now. *That's where all the secrets are …*

And the land's screaming stopped. For one glorious moment, she was surrounded in the hush of perfect silence. Then the sound of bells exploded all around her, ringing with glorious certainty.

Air gathered tangibly behind her, ready to push her forward if she wavered.

That way. Go!

'Connall told me where to go next,' she said. 'We need to find Raven's Nest.'

They were still arguing ten minutes later, as all three stood on the high hilltop gazing down through thick sapphire air at the vast kingdom spread before them. It was all so much *bigger* than Cordelia had expected! Farms and marshes and high-walled towns dotted the dark landscape, along with burned-out fields and ruined castles rotting in broken solitude. Silver rivers snaked across the horizon, while tiny wounded woodlands clumped in patches.

In the distance, Cordelia glimpsed a line of moving shadows that might have been another army, marching.

There was *so much* waiting for them in the land beyond, like it or not … and a line of high mountains rose beyond all the rest, their distant peaks hidden by clouds.

'So Raven's Nest is just "up in the mountains", eh?' Rosalind waved furiously at the horizon. 'Well, *that'll* be easy to find, then. Just an hour or two of wandering around, d'you think, before we'll spot it? Or maybe a *month or two*? While we leave the others to rot so we can *chat with* a bunch of mythical spirits who might not even exist any more?' Her voice rose to a roaring bellow.

'Connall said—' began Cordelia.

'Connall *isn't here*,' Rosalind spat. 'If we do what *you* want, he never will be again! B*ah!*' Rolling her eyes, she stomped down the other side of the hill and disappeared into the growing shadows.

There was green grass on that side of the hill. There were knotted tree roots too, and tangles of brambles that swarmed treacherously across the ground. A moment after Rosalind had disappeared, a loud *thump* sounded through the evening air. The grumbling that came afterwards was even louder as Rosalind picked herself up from her fall.

Giles sighed. 'We'd better give her a minute to cool down.'

The argument still seethed, unresolved among them, as they all staggered and slid down the far side of the hill in the deepening darkness, bumping into stones and roots and brambles along the way. Cordelia's head was still full of those looming, impossible mountains, and her whole body ached with the remnants of those final screams from the brown land they'd escaped. She didn't dare turn animal again, not yet – not even to see better in the dark. She couldn't bear to be separated from her triplets again, not even simply in her shape.

It was a relief to hear birds rustling nearby at their bumbling movements, and to catch the soft whisper of a fox slipping past them. At least this part of the land hadn't broken.

So many burned-out patches across the kingdom ...

Would their own forest look like that when the dukes were through with it?

'Oi, Cordy.' Catching up, Giles bumped her arm companionably with his. 'Can you guess what I'm thinking about?'

Cordelia rolled her eyes, glad to be shaken out of the dark forest of her thoughts. 'Food? As usual?'

'Even better. This would make a *perfect* ballad. Admit it! The three of us questing to save our family; one of us *maybe* ending up as the king or queen—'

'No!' Cordelia flinched, stumbling to a halt in the darkness. 'No one can stay king or queen while the Raven Crown is broken – and Connall says they've all given up on even trying to fix it. Anyone who gets pushed on to that throne now will *die*.'

'Well, a lot of the best ballads do have tragic endings.' Giles gave a melodramatic sigh, his voice turning into a soft, lilting croon. 'I could be *the great lost king, the flower of the land, the fairest son who e'er sung—*'

Cordelia snarled, 'That isn't funny!'

Bracing herself against the call of the land around her, she shifted into wolf form after all and loped ahead to scout for hidden dangers in the night.

Giles's voice floated plaintively after her. 'Has anyone spotted any berries we could eat yet?'

Cordelia scented no berries on that dark, tangled hillside. Further down, though, she scented plenty of people – and danger too, waiting for the triplets at the bottom of the hill.

A camp of humans was hiding near the bottom of the hill, taking shelter within a patch of pine trees. They were speaking in whispers too low for Cordelia to catch, but the scent of aggression floating through the air was unmistakable.

'Bandits,' Rosalind pronounced, when Cordelia ran back to the others to report. She had been scowling and muttering to herself when Cordelia arrived, but she brightened at this news, and started scouring the ground in the darkness for a new sword-stick. 'Lying in wait for rich travellers to pass, I'd guess.'

'They're out of luck with *us*, then,' said Giles. 'We don't even have any food for them to steal. Do you think we should warn them we're bad pickings? I could sing very loudly about how much my stomach's rumbling. I've been practising a song about it in my head for the last few hours.'

'I expect I'll just have to fight them off.' Rosalind straightened, holding a fallen branch, and started busily stripping off the leaves. 'Don't worry, Giles. You can write an even better ballad about that. In the meantime, though, I don't want either of you hurt – so, you stand back and hide with Cordy while I take care of all the fighting.'

'What? No!' Giles squawked. 'Why would you pick a fight with grown-up *bandits*? That makes no sense! You don't even have a real sword!'

Cordelia didn't bother to argue. She just shifted into bear shape, big and clawed, looming over both of them ... and not about to hide from *anyone*.

Rosalind shook her head pityingly. 'Oh, I know you *look* fierce now, Cordy. But if any of those bandits had ever practised wrestling with you—'

Cordelia growled down at her arrogant sister and lifted her muzzle in a sneer.

'Couldn't we just walk a different way and avoid them?' Giles was still protesting as Rosalind stalked down the hillside five minutes later with Cordelia padding in her wake. He followed well behind them both, streaming complaints at his sisters with every lagging step. 'If we only went *around* instead—'

'They probably have lookouts waiting to ambush travellers at several different points.' Rosalind didn't even slow her confident stride. 'Best to face them head-on so we know exactly where they are.'

'But what *travellers* could they be waiting for?' Giles tripped over a rock, but it didn't slow his argument. 'How many travellers ever come out of our forest? We're the only ones who live there!'

'Well, then maybe they're hoping to kidnap their new queen.' Rosalind smacked her stick menacingly against her side. 'We'll see how they like the ransom *we'll* give them!'

'But—'

'*Who goes there?*' It was a man's warning shout, high and angry.

Cordelia's bear nose caught something unexpected in the air: the scent of fear beneath the anger. She tilted her big shaggy head, sniffing harder.

Why would ferocious bandits be frightened of any passers-by?

'Stand back if you value your lives, villains!' Rosalind shouted. 'You'll regret it if you try to face *us* down, I promise you!'

Giles let out a heartfelt groan.

Cordelia huffed warningly at her sister. There was more going on here than they'd realised …

But as usual, Rosalind was barrelling ahead without bothering to ask any questions first. 'Lay down your weapons, *now!*' she bellowed.

'Never!' the man bellowed back. Agitated rustling sounded in the trees – more humans hurrying to take up places behind him. Metal clanked ominously. Voices whispered. Fear filled the air.

And then—

Cordelia couldn't have caught it with human ears: the sound of a hastily muffled cry.

Wait. There were other children here. Babies too – she could smell them. *That* was why these strangers were afraid! They were hiding in the dark, trying to protect their own families.

'Come on, Cordy.' Rosalind started forward. '*Attack!*'

The strangers started towards them in return.

Cordelia slammed herself in front of Rosalind in her big bear form. Then she shifted back into a girl. The shock of her transformation made the adults jerk back, breaths hissing loudly through their teeth.

Rosalind's mouth dropped open too. 'What are you doing?' she hissed. 'You can't do us any good like *that!*'

It was true that Cordelia had no claws in girl form. But she needed distraction, not physical strength, to defuse this particular battle … and luckily, she knew someone who was *always* happy to be the centre of attention.

'Giles,' she said, 'you can sing us that ballad now.'

It was the moment that Giles had been born for. As Cordelia watched in awe – and Rosalind groaned in despair – he flung both long arms out in a dramatic flourish and bounded to the centre of the confrontation.

Both sisters knew exactly what that deep indrawn breath heralded.

'*My stomach!*' His bell-like voice pealed at top volume through the air, throbbing with intensity and sending onlookers lurching involuntarily backwards. '*Oh, the tale of my stomach is a tale of woe, of pain even greater than my throbbing toe …*'

On every side, weapons lowered as strangers stared in slack-jawed disbelief. Metal glinted in their hands, the source of those earlier clanking noises – but it was the metal of spades and weed hooks, not martial swords or spears. Cordelia pointed them out, wordlessly, to Rosalind – who scowled more ferociously than ever.

'*… For berries are few, and now I rue that I never ate more of Alys's stew …*'

'He *couldn't* have eaten any more of it,' Rosalind muttered under her breath to Cordelia. 'He would have burst!'

'... And *now that we're here, I greatly fear that I may well shed more than one*—'

'What is going on?' A tall, broad-shouldered older girl with skin a darker brown than Connall's shoved past all the staring adults and held up a flickering candle to light the scene. 'Where are those ferocious *bandits* you were ordering us all to hide from, Hal?'

'They ... well ...' The blond, bearded man who'd shouted back and forth with Rosalind shook his head now, blinking rapidly as he turned to face the new arrival. 'This lot threatened us, Tilda, so we had to—'

'*Threatened* you?' She took one sweeping look across the group. 'For goodness' sake, they're only *children*!'

Rosalind opened her mouth with a furious huff of air. Cordelia kicked her, hard.

Luckily, Tilda wasn't looking at them any more.

'What were you thinking?' she demanded of the armed group. 'Or did those dukes claim your eyes as well as all our farms?' Shaking her head in disgust, she turned back to Cordelia, Rosalind and Giles. 'You poor things. Did we frighten you horribly?'

'*He* didn't seem frightened,' a different woman

muttered behind her, pointing at Giles. 'He's just thinking about his stomach!'

'Aren't we all?' Tilda sighed, beckoning Giles closer. 'You certainly have an impressive voice, lad. I'm sorry it was wasted on an unappreciative audience.'

Rosalind snorted. Cordelia rolled her eyes.

Giles gave her a fabulous bow. 'At your service, milady,' he said grandly. 'I'm afraid we've been lost in the forest for some time. It was lonely and frightening – and there weren't enough berries, as I may have mentioned – and my sisters are both terribly excitable, so—'

'The forest?' Tilda took a rapid step back, pulling her ragged shawl tighter around her shoulders. 'You went into the *enchanted* forest? By yourselves? Why would you ever do such a foolish thing?'

'Ah …' Giles faltered, and Hal seized his chance.

'*She* was a bear!' he said, pointing at Cordelia. 'I saw her! She—no, she really *was*, Tilda!' he added plaintively, as she turned to give him a severe look. 'Those soldiers *told* us to watch out for demons from the forest. And everyone here can tell you too! We *all* saw her change shape … didn't we?'

Whispers and mumbles circled round the men as Tilda tilted her candle to look each one of them in the face.

'It was dark,' another man said weakly. 'I thought …
but I mean, I suppose I *might* have—'

'She doesn't look like a bear to *me*,' said Tilda. 'You're
seeing spectres in the shadows, and you should know
better, at your ages! But *you* children,' she added sternly to
Giles, 'should never have done anything so wild and reck-
less! Your poor parents must be—'

'Our father is dead,' said Rosalind flatly. 'Our mother
was in the forest with us.'

'Ohhh.' She breathed out the word, exchanging a look
with the men and women around her. 'Was she one of the
soldiers forced inside to face that wicked enchantress? Oh,
you poor things. No wonder—!'

She cut herself off, wincing. 'Never mind. You're safe
with us for the night, at least. This lot won't leave so much
as a sparrow unchallenged. You can have a good sleep
before you make any decisions about what to do next. I
only wish—'

'We need to go to Raven's Nest,' said Cordelia, just as
Rosalind said ominously, '*Wicked enchantress?*'

'Shut up, shut up, shut up!' Giles hissed at Rosalind.
To Cordelia, he added urgently, 'We haven't actually
decided—'

'Can you tell us where it is?' Cordelia focused on
Tilda, shutting out all the others' nonsense. 'All we know is

that it's somewhere up in the mountains. But it looks like there are a lot of those.'

'A ... lot of mountains?' Tilda shook her head, sounding dazed. 'I think we'd better sit down and talk all this over. But first ...' She glanced at Giles as his stomach let out a loud and unmistakable growl. 'Let's find something to fill that stomach before *it* starts singing to us too.'

15

Strangers and new surroundings were exactly the distraction that Cordelia needed to get her mind off her own fears. Her triplets followed Tilda's directions to sit and wait by a small flickering campfire surrounded by blankets where half a dozen other children slept. Cordelia, though, followed Tilda through the small camp, soaking up every new sight and sound along the way. It was all so different from her forest!

Adults bustled and clustered on all sides, talking in worried groups, comforting cranky babies, or – in the case of four of the men – arguing in heated undertones. As she watched, the grouchy one called Hal threw up his hands in visible disgust and stomped off, ducking under the low-hanging branches of the closest tree and disappearing into the deep shadows beyond.

'Where did you all come from?' Cordelia asked, trying in vain to peer after him. Human eyes were so useless when it came to seeing in the dark! 'Or do you live here normally?'

'Live *here*?' Tilda snorted as she slid between two groups of women sitting on the open ground, holding her own empty jug close to her chest. 'Does this *look* like a home to you?'

It didn't look like Cordelia's castle, or even Lady Elianora's cottage. But then, no one here looked the way she was used to. Their clothes weren't the tunics or armour of the dukes' soldiers, but they weren't made of the richly coloured fabrics that Alys and Mother had always sewn with, either. They looked rough and plain, and the people who wore them looked as if they'd been tired and worried for ages.

'No, our homes were stolen by those *dukes*.' Tilda snapped out her last word like a curse as she came to a halt by a pile of baskets.

The red-haired older girl who sat guard by the baskets, wrapped in a fraying shawl, frowned up at her. 'You've already taken your share for your family.'

'*She* hasn't.' Tilda pointed at Cordelia.

The girl wrinkled her nose in distaste. 'They're not locals.'

'And we're not dukes or duchesses. We *care* about people who aren't our own, remember?' Tilda put her hands on her hips as the older girl hesitated. 'They're *children*, Margery. Look at them! We can't let them go hungry.'

'We'll all go hungry soon enough if we aren't careful,' Margery muttered. Still, she shifted aside to make room. 'Just don't give them any of our meat. We don't have enough of that to spare on outsiders.'

Tilda sighed, but she didn't argue. 'Here.' She reached into the closest basket and ripped off a thick chunk of bread. 'You can carry this.' She handed it to Cordelia, then bent to fill her cracked china jug from the tall bucket of water that stood by the baskets. 'This'll have to do, for now.'

It took all Cordelia's patience to wait until they had left the other girl behind before she let more of her questions pour out. 'What do you mean, the dukes stole your homes? Don't they have their own homes to live in?'

'Oh, they wouldn't dream of living in our little farms! But they wanted somewhere to house their armies. And according to *them* –' Tilda let out a humourless laugh, her stride lengthening – 'they were doing it all for our own good. The Duke of Lune's woman told us we were *honoured* to pack up our things and begone so we could provide them with a safe base to invade the forest and protect us all from the wicked enchantress.'

'What? *Why?*' Cordelia scowled, hurrying to keep up. 'She wasn't attacking you.'

'Of course not!' Tilda lowered her voice to an angry murmur as they neared the campfire where the other children slept and where Giles and Rosalind sat, chatting softly to each other. 'We're not fools. We've always been safe from her as long as we didn't venture into her forest. *They* don't care about our safety. It was just a useful excuse. And that duke's messenger may have promised all sorts of rewards if we catch any of the witch's terrible demons trying to escape –' she rolled her eyes meaningfully – 'but we *all* know what's really coming.'

She handed the water jug to Rosalind, her free hand fisting by her side. 'Now their armies are sprawled across our fields, ruining all this year's crops, and we'll never get our own homes back again. They'll be divided among the dukes' knights as rewards for their loyalty.'

Rosalind straightened with outrage. 'That's not fair! They can't just steal people's farms and livelihoods! A true knight would *never*—'

'A *true knight*? Who's ever seen one of those?' Tilda let out a scornful laugh. 'I don't know what strange country you three come from beyond that awful forest, but the men and women who rule *this* kingdom don't give a turnip for knightly honour. All they care about is

135

power … and none of us have enough of *that* to fight back against them.'

She sighed as she sat down, folding the coarse skirts of her smock around her. 'My mother said that in the old days, they all had to listen to the king or queen … but *that* ended decades ago, back when the Raven Crown first broke. Now, it doesn't even matter which duke or duchess grabs the throne for their family. The others are always ready to knock them off and start the bloodshed all over again. We're just the pieces that get smashed along the way.'

A look came over Giles's face that Cordelia knew only too well. He was coming up with a new song; no doubt something grand and hopelessly melancholy, his very favourite type. 'So the Dukes of Arden and Lune –' he glanced sidelong at his sisters – 'are fighting together for the House of Harcourt's heir to the Raven Throne? But the Duchess of Solenne and the Dukes of Breville and Mordaunt all want a different heir to win so that *they* can seize power for themselves instead? And it's all doomed to epic tragedy forever?'

Cordelia glared at him through slitted eyes. '*Don't even think about singing*,' she hissed.

There was nothing grand or ballad-worthy about a war that broke apart the land and stole people's homes to fight over a stupid throne. More than that—

'Our *father* was killed in one of those battles,' she muttered, 'before we were even born. Our older brother's father was killed in another.'

Both of her triplets jerked around to gape at her. She hunched her shoulders against the look of shock on Giles's face. She hadn't been keeping Connall's story a *secret* from the others; she simply hadn't had the chance to share all of it with them yet.

Wings itched to explode from her shoulder blades and fly her away. She dug the fingers of her left hand into her legs to hold herself down as she shoved the bread at Giles to share out. 'What about Raven's Nest?' she asked Tilda. 'Where is that?'

'That wasn't just a strange jest earlier?' Tilda's frowning gaze lifted from her hands. 'Raven's Nest is a fairy tale. A legend.'

'Oh, really?' Giles perked up, stuffing a chunk of bread into his mouth and handing the rest to Rosalind. 'Please do tell us, then. I love legends!'

'*You* only want to write more songs.' Rosalind ripped the remaining bread in half. 'But if this means we don't actually have to go questing after mythical nonsense—'

'No,' said Cordelia. 'It's a real place. We just need to find it.'

'Hmm,' said Tilda. 'Well in all the *stories* people tell, it's hidden near the top of Mount Corve, surrounded by clouds and unnatural mist and barred against anyone without magic or royal blood. It holds *all* the mysteries and secrets of the past, and the Raven Crown is waiting there to be mended one day by its true and rightful heir.

'And if you think no one's ever tried to make *that* come true—!' She let out a dismissive huff of air. 'Those nobles have been shedding *everyone's* blood for decades, and they have plenty of magic on their side.'

Cordelia leaned closer, ignoring the piece of stale bread in her hand. 'Which mountain is Mount Corve?'

'Oh, the tallest of them all, of course – smack dab in the centre of the range. That's probably what made the legend stick in the first place.' Tilda shrugged. 'It *looks* like the sort of place that ought to be magic, if you're the sort of person who believes in pretty fairy tales and lost legends. I've certainly never known anyone with magic to help anyone besides themselves.'

Her eyes narrowed as she leaned forward too, until she and Cordelia were almost nose-to-nose. 'But why do you even want to know? And where did you three come from, anyway? People were telling each other that tale long before any of us were born. How could you never have heard it before – especially when you're so determined to go there?'

Before Cordelia could answer, there was a shout from one of the women who stood guard by the edge of the trees. 'Soldiers coming!'

The camp erupted into chaos. Cordelia leaped to her feet along with everyone else. Voices rose in confusion and fear as adults raced to gather up the other children from their rest.

Tilda called out urgently, 'Are they coming from the forest? Is the enchantress with them?'

'No, they're coming from the farms, seven men-at-arms together—wait! Hal's with them. He's leading them here!'

'*What?*' Tilda's mouth dropped open. 'But why? Oh, *no*. How could he be so stupid – and so *cruel*?'

'What's going on?' Scooping up her sword-stick, Rosalind took up a martial stance just ahead of Cordelia and Giles.

'He's told the soldiers about you three!' Tilda groaned. 'They asked us to watch out for demons, and he swore he'd seen your sister transform from a bear – but how he could really believe—argh! He must have thought, if he only pleased them, they would give him back his farm. That *fool*!'

'Quickly. They'll be here any moment!' A fair-haired older woman hurried up, a whimpering baby pressed firmly against her shoulder. 'Can we hide these three?'

'Not if Hal's here to find them. They could run—'

'They won't get away. Not now.' The silver-haired man who spoke was holding a spade raised and ready in his knobbly brown hands, but his shoulders sagged as if they'd already been defeated. 'Tilda ... if we try to protect these poor children, who will protect *our* grandchildren?'

'*Don't* try to protect us.' Rosalind glared into the shadows beyond the trees, where faint clanking sounds could already be heard. She raised her sword-stick threateningly. 'We'll take care of ourselves.'

Giles was shivering visibly, but for once, he didn't disagree. 'We're truly sorry for any trouble we've brought upon you.' His voice wobbled, losing all its vibrant performing strength. 'None of us ever wanted that to happen.'

'But ... no!' Tilda shook her head fiercely, wrapping her arms around her chest. 'I can't bear it. We've let them take so much already. To just stand here and watch *children* be stolen, without even trying to protect them—!'

'We won't be taken.' Cold certainty formed in Cordelia's chest as she stepped back, finding a clear patch of ground. 'No one here needs a battle,' she told her triplets. 'They just need us *gone* for their own safety.'

'How?' Tilda demanded. 'Even if you run back towards that awful forest, you'll never outrace them. You're only half their size!'

Cordelia looked up at Tilda's desperately braced body ... and at the hungry people all around them, with nothing more than spades and plant hooks to defend themselves from the dukes' armed soldiers.

... Her family's soldiers, whether she liked it or not.

Rosalind was right: None of this was fair.

'We'll lead them away from you,' Cordelia promised, 'and we will help you if we ever can.'

Rosalind jerked a nod. 'We certainly *will*.'

Giles gave Tilda a weak smile. 'You'll be in my songs too, from now on – and you won't ever be forgotten.'

Cordelia turned horse in a single violent lunge of power. The ragged group around her gasped and stumbled back in shock.

The big muscles in her haunches flexed. She shook back her thick mane and let out a high trumpeting neigh that echoed across the landscape in furious challenge to all attackers. Her triplets scrambled swiftly up on to her lofty black back ...

And she lunged forward, breaking through the last of the shadowy trees to gallop past the marching soldiers and across the wide, flat fields beyond, with shouts and angry clanks of armour pursuing them into the night.

16

Being a horse was fantastically useful. Once the soldiers were left behind, Cordelia slowed to a steady ground-covering trot. It wasn't long after that before Rosalind and Giles started calling out for her to stop – but with both of them safely trapped on her back, none of their noisy threats made any difference.

By the time she finally collapsed by a stream, panting and trembling and drenched with sweat, they were miles closer to Raven's Nest.

'That was a low trick!' Rosalind landed on the ground with a groan and rolled immediately on to her back, eyes falling shut. 'Tomorrow ...' Her voice broke into a yawn. 'Tomorrow I'll tell you *exactly* ...'

But Cordelia was busy slurping up fresh cold water with her long snout stuck into the stream. She paid no attention to Rosalind's dire predictions or complaints. They faded away soon enough, shifting into loud rattling snores.

There. Her triplets were both safe, and they were all heading exactly where they needed to go.

Giles didn't fall asleep so quickly, though. He sat beside Cordelia on the grass, one hand resting on her skin as she drank. He was strangely quiet as he sat there, in a way that might have worried her if she hadn't been so tired. When she raised her head from the water at last, the only sounds in the pre-dawn darkness were the soft burbles of the stream as it flowed past and Rosalind's snores rising beside them.

The soft grass smelt delicious, but Cordelia was too exhausted even to nose around and eat it. She had run as long and as far as she could, well beyond her new body's limits of endurance. Now she tucked up her long legs and prepared to fall flat on to her side for the few remaining hours of darkness.

Giles's voice stopped her. 'I know you're keeping secrets from us.' He didn't look away from the rippling dark water, but his fingers tightened against her. 'Even Ros'll figure that out soon enough.'

With a sigh of surrender, Cordelia slipped back into girl form. Cold, damp grass poked through her dress. Her human head ached.

'I'm not keeping any secrets you need to know,' she whispered softly. 'I'll tell you everything Connall said about our father – and about Mother too.'

'So *Connall* isn't the one who upset you. I knew it!' Giles's whisper vibrated with intensity. 'Cordy, Grandmother's our family just as much as yours. I *know* she turned out to be awful. You saved us, and I'm grateful for it! But whatever she said that you've been burning up about ever since – we deserve to hear it too.

'And when it comes to Raven's Nest – I don't believe for one second that *Connall* wanted us to go questing halfway across the kingdom to some mythical, dangerous place in the mountains. I know our brother – so I *know* he must have told you we should hide and stay safe. Didn't he?'

Cordelia's shoulders hunched. 'He *did* tell me about Raven's Nest – and he said the spirits there hold all the deepest secrets in the land. If they can share any of those secrets with us – if they can tell us what we need to know to get Mother and the others free, and who ... Well, we just *have* to go, Giles! It's our only chance to save our family.'

'But you didn't take the time to talk us into it. You just dragged us here against our will.' Giles shook his head grimly. 'You can't shut us out and make all the decisions! Otherwise, you're acting just like Mother – and at least I trusted *her* to make those decisions for our own good.'

His words stabbed into Cordelia's chest. *Was* she imitating everything that had always outraged her in Mother?

She *was* keeping secrets from the others. But she couldn't help it! If she told Giles the other question that was hissing and coiling like a viper in her chest, it would change everything. She couldn't bear it.

She *needed* a real answer from those spirits, or Grandmother's words would poison everything for good.

'We only have each other now, Cordy. Just the three of us.' Giles let out a shuddering sigh. 'If I can't even trust my own sisters any more ...'

'You're not even their real sister.'

She would *never* tell him that!

In a heartbeat, Cordelia was a horse again. She tipped her big body over and fell flat on her side, whiffling air pointedly through her lips. Horses didn't have to answer questions. Even Giles couldn't talk forever to an animal who wouldn't answer back.

When he finally did fall silent, though, he stood up and moved three feet away from her before curling up on Rosalind's far side ... and Cordelia felt every inch of the new distance he had put between them.

The next morning, Cordelia woke to find her siblings huddled together, whispering to each other with their backs turned against her. The sight felt *wrong* – as painfully off-kilter as the fractured land that had creaked and moaned its misery into her dreams, leaving her fragile and desperate for comfort. Still sleep-fogged and aching in every muscle, Cordelia rolled up from the grass and shook herself off in preparation to shift back into girl form and join them.

Then she looked down and froze.

Tiny white starflowers dotted the grass where she had lain, springing up to catch the early morning light.

Sharp, cold fear pierced her chest as she stared down at them.

Coincidence?

No. They formed a perfect outline – but not of the big horse-body she wore. In the grass, she could see the outline of the small girl-body that was her true form.

Remembered voices whispered in her ears: '*You are ours and always have been.*'

No. *I'm not! I won't be! I have a family!* She stumbled backwards, tripping over all four long legs.

Her triplets both turned at her movement. Their flat, identical expressions halted her mid-tangle, her mind still racing in panicked, useless circles.

'You win,' said Giles grimly. 'We're going to Raven's Nest because you're our sister and we *want* to trust you.

But once we get there, you have to tell us everything. That is the only bargain that either of us will agree to.'

He stalked off to wash his face and hands in the stream, while Rosalind strode off in the opposite direction to stand guard without a word … and the delicate white starflowers waved in the morning breeze, a silent but unmistakable reminder.

Even the land knew that Cordelia didn't really fit in with the others, no matter how hard she tried to hide.

She stayed in horse form for the rest of that morning, even when they stopped for rests. Neither of her triplets asked her to change back. They only spoke to each other. They barely even looked at her.

It was exactly what she'd wanted. No *arguments*. No *interference*. She didn't have to share any terrifying truths.

If she had been a wolf, she would have *bitten* them. Hard!

She trotted instead on long, strong legs, hooves pounding against the rutted dirt roads that stretched past abandoned farms and watchtowers. Half the crops had been left rotting in the fields, while burned-out husks of stone buildings rose like skeletons nearby. Rosalind's legs clamped tighter and tighter around Cordelia's back with every new wreck that they passed, while Giles hummed a low, unhappy melody, gangly legs twitching in time with his wordless tune of discontent.

From time to time, his voice echoed around them from random angles as he practised more of the sorcery he'd managed in the forest – but at least half the time, the sound faded within seconds. The rest of the time, it didn't emerge at all.

'It's no use!' Panting hard, he slumped over Cordelia's neck. 'I can't do it on command. I should have stuck with Mother's training after all!'

At that, Cordelia snorted grumpily through her muzzle. Atop her back, Rosalind made just as sceptical a sound. '*You* always said you'd dry up into a husk if we didn't let you spend enough time singing. Remember?'

'It's true,' he mumbled dolefully, 'but at least then I'd have some way of being *useful*. Cordy can turn herself into a lion. *You* know how to fight with weapons. I don't even have a lute here to mistune! What am I supposed to do the next time we're attacked if I can't figure out how to use my magic? *Sing* a bunch of soldiers into giving up?'

If Cordelia had been in girl form, she would have laughed at that image. But she couldn't speak through her horse muzzle, and after a long silence, Rosalind said, 'Who do you think is going to attack us?'

'Oh, I don't know. There are too many possibilities!'

He laughed painfully against Cordelia's mane, his shoulders shaking. 'The Dukes of Lune and Arden, maybe? *They* want to force one of us on to the throne just so they can run the kingdom for themselves. But if we're unlucky enough to stumble across the Duchess of Solenne or her allies, they'll want us dead to get us out of the way of their own heir. Oh, and then there's that wicked sorceress grandmother of ours who wants to trade us to the dukes in our own family!'

He let out a heavy sigh that ruffled against Cordelia's skin. 'Arden and Lune, at least, must know by now that we've left the forest. It's not as if anyone else could have been those three children who came running out and got spotted by *everyone* along the way.'

Rosalind grunted. 'That man who reported us to the soldiers thought we were demons.'

'Ha.' Drawing a deep breath, Giles straightened in his seat. 'I don't think the dukes will be so easily fooled.'

Grandmother wouldn't be fooled either, if she heard. Cordelia chewed over that thought unhappily as she trotted onwards, dust kicking up around every step.

Grandmother hadn't had any stables behind her cottage to hold a horse ready to ride. She certainly couldn't catch up with them by foot.

But Cordelia remembered the blaze in those dark eyes – 'I've *had twelve years to learn from my mistakes.*'

Even in horse form, she shivered hard.

Lady Elianora would never give up at her first setback … and next time, she wouldn't be nearly so easy to surprise.

17

The attacks that Giles had predicted didn't come that day, though, or the next.

Soldiers on horseback swept up and down the road four different times as they journeyed. The triplets found hiding places every time. They skirted around high-walled towns surrounded by massive stinking piles of refuse and rivers polluted with the townsfolk's leavings. Army camps sprawled across abandoned fields. The flags that flew above those camps shifted symbols and colours as the long days passed, but the devastation left behind was universal.

It was no wonder the land was crying out for mercy.

Colourful flags of boars, badgers and falcons flew high in triumph above the latest field of dying crops. Cordelia bared her teeth when she saw them: the symbols of Lune's and Arden's rivals, the Duchess of Solenne and her allies, who all wanted a different heir for the Raven Throne … and who would kill Cordelia and her triplets to achieve that goal.

They can have the stupid throne, she thought bitterly. But, of course, it made no difference what she thought. Lune and Arden wouldn't listen even if all three triplets begged on their knees to give it up. All *they* cared about was seizing power for themselves … and keeping the Duchess of Solenne's alternate heir from gaining it.

Who *was* that other possible heir, anyway? Would *they* care about this broken kingdom?

Someone had to do something, for the sake of every innocent pawn in the dukes' and duchesses' schemes … and for the sake of the land itself, whose pitiful moans echoed endlessly through Cordelia's ears.

Broken. Broken. Broken!

The triplets camped out of sight of the farmhouses that still stood. They foraged for their food in abandoned fields. They didn't talk to anyone else along their journey … but then, after everything they saw on their first day, they barely even spoke to one another.

The only sound that accompanied them across the miles, apart from the steady thumping of Cordelia's hooves along the road, was the mournful tune that Giles hummed to himself over and over throughout the days. For once, neither of his sisters asked him to stop. Its melancholy lilt perfectly echoed the wreckage that they passed.

Rosalind brooded in dangerous silence, her body growing more and more rigid atop Cordelia's back with every burned-out castle or farm that they passed. Cordelia stayed animal and tried with all her might to shut out the cries of the land around her ... but every night in her dreams, they wrung her out and left her reeling, groggy and half deafened by endless screams, pleas and demands.

BROKEN. BROKEN. DO SOMETHING!

And every night as she slept, white starflowers grew beneath her in her true shape, as if to taunt her. *We know what you truly are.*

This wounded land expected her to somehow *fix* it. Mother, Connall and Alys needed her to rescue them from their powerful captors. And with every step towards that highest cloud-wreathed mountain, she was drawing closer to the moment when she would have to let her own most terrible words out into the air, to fulfil the bargain that her triplets had demanded.

Then they would finally know the truth about her, and—

No!

She couldn't even let herself think it.

She kept her eyes trained on the thickly forested slopes of Mount Corve as they drew closer with every passing minute. She kept her hooves moving steadily as she trotted up steep, sloping dirt roads and around jutting boulders, and she squeezed her inner ears shut as hard as she could to the cries of the land on every side.

So she almost missed the trap that was waiting for them.

The closer the triplets came to Mount Corve, the more the landscape rippled with obstacles, like giant shoulders rising from the earth to shrug off irritating human invaders. Every time Cordelia made it to the top of one slippery loose-soiled hill with her triplets still safely clinging to her back, she found yet another hill waiting between her and that high green mountain like an endless series of tests that she had to pass.

But she couldn't keep moving forever. As the sun blazed in a cloudless sky above them, they all stopped, yet again, to eat and rest for a solid hour. They were so painfully close to Mount Corve by then that Cordelia could have wept with frustration at the delay – but her legs were trembling uncontrollably. Her endurance as a horse was so paltry!

She dutifully filled her stomach with fresh grass but then turned girl, flopping back against the rocky hill where they'd stopped while Giles and Rosalind wandered off to forage. The three of them had left behind the last signs of human habitation over an hour earlier, and for once, there was no sign of any devastation to explain it. Apparently, no humans had ever dared to build this close to Mount Corve, much less hold any battles here.

The land here felt dangerously unsettled beneath Cordelia's body. All across the kingdom, as hard as she'd tried not to pay any attention, she had *felt* the transition in each patch of land they'd crossed, like multiple pieces of a larger patchwork quilt – all of them sewn together into a whole, but each one individual and distinct. Each area held its own particular chorus of voices … and its own vivid history of pain.

This chunk of land, just by Mount Corve, wasn't screaming like so many others had along the way. It wasn't even calling for her attention. Instead, it felt somehow as if it were … waiting.

Holding its breath?

As she lay on the sloping grass and dirt, her eyes shut to bask in the warm sunshine, she found herself scratching again and again with one finger at the side of her head. There was a subtle tickle of sensation there, inside her ear, like a squirrel trying to sneakily scratch its way through a door, or …

No! It was the land itself trying to wriggle through her defences. She sat up with a jerk, shaking herself off vigorously. *I'm not listening! I won't hear you!*

'... *was a time ... could come agai*—Cordy!' Giles's song cut off as he rounded the hill, his eyes widening as he watched her shuddering movements. 'Is everything all right?'

'It's. *Fine.*' She gritted out the words, using all her energy to hold her inner defences strong.

She *wouldn't* let the land distract her now; wouldn't let it separate her from her triplets in these last few hours before the truth came between the three of them.

'Are you sure?' He frowned, starting towards her. 'If you're not feeling well—'

'I said I'm *fine!*' She bared her teeth in a ferocious forced smile. 'Why don't you keep singing? I can listen to your new song.'

He paled behind his freckles. 'Ros!' he yelled. 'There's something wrong with Cordy!'

'Ha, ha. Very funny.' Rolling her eyes, Cordelia pushed herself to her feet. Every muscle in her body ached with the effort she'd been through ... and when she looked down at the grass where she'd lain, she spotted a single white starflower poking its head up through the green.

She jerked backwards as if it were an adder preparing to strike.

'What's wrong with Cordy?' Rosalind rounded the hill at a run.

Giles pointed at Cordelia accusingly. 'She said she *wants* to hear me sing.'

Snorting, Rosalind slowed to a halt. 'Has she lost her hearing? Or only her mind?'

'Oh, *shut up*, both of you!' Cordelia backed hastily away from the tell-tale flower. 'Let's just get moving.'

'*Can* you? Already?' Rosalind frowned, catching up and peering into her face suspiciously. 'I thought you needed more rest than that. Horses—'

'I can't carry either of you,' Cordelia mumbled, 'but I *can* walk on my own two legs. And it's not as if we're far from Mount Corve. So there's no point waiting any longer, is there?'

Giles looked more than ready to offer *several* points, quite possibly set to music, so Cordelia turned her back on them both and started forward without letting her brother's loud groan of frustration – or her own aching legs – stop her.

She could *feel* that starflower waving mockingly in the breeze behind her.

As they trudged further and further up and down the rocky paths through the bumpy foothills, the voice of the land beneath her feet stopped subtly scratching at her ear and started hammering outright at her head instead. She clenched her jaw tight. *La-la-la – I can't hear you!*

Her triplets were talking again now, in low, worried tones, about what dangers might lie ahead. She tried to listen to them – she really did. But the voices of the land formed an angry blur in her ears, all demand and distress and something sharp at the edges almost like a warning, and—

'What do you think, Cordy?'

'Sorry?' Breathing hard, she blinked out at her siblings. Only one more slope rose before them now until they would reach the real mountain at last.

… Where everything would change.

Giles stared at her. 'Who *were* you listening to, just then?'

'*Nobody,*' she snarled – then caught herself. 'I mean, you?'

Rosalind let out a huff of a laugh. 'Nice try. She was off in her own world, as usual.'

'No!' Cordelia said. 'I'm right here. With *you*.' She forced herself to meet her sister's gaze full on, even as the voices in her head rose to ear-piercing screams. 'I just—'

SOLDIERS AHEAD!

She doubled over, her vision whiting out with pain as the combined voices smashed through her internal walls.

'Cordy!'

'What's happening?'

'Stop,' she gasped. 'Wait! We can't. Go any further. *Soldiers!* Waiting for us.'

Her head throbbed with agony. She clutched it with both hands, desperately filtering through all the different competing visions.

'The mist –' she panted – 'a wall of mist – they're so close now … No, they're waiting right in front of it. *Lying* in wait! They know we're coming.'

'How could they possibly know that?' Rosalind demanded.

'Oh … I know the answer to that question.' Giles's weary sigh ruffled against Cordelia's tangled hair. 'Remember? The very first moment we met those farmers, Cordy asked them how to get to Raven's Nest. The farmer who reported us to the soldiers must have told them about that too.'

'So that's where the real attack is waiting.' Rosalind smacked her sword-stick against one palm with a *thwack!* '*They* think we're walking into a trap.'

'We almost did.' Giles's voice tightened. 'The real question is, how did *Cordy* know about it?'

Cordelia couldn't answer. She could barely even breathe. Now that the land had forced its way back into her head, that old hook inside her chest was back as well.

At home, it had only tugged her to escape her castle walls, to escape into the freedom and the wildness outside – but this time, it had a more specific goal in mind.

It *yanked*, again and again. A whimper of pain huffed through her throat.

Her right foot moved forward against her will.

Rosalind grabbed hold of her arm. 'Wait up! You can't fight them when you're like this.'

'Who wants to fight trained soldiers at *all*?' Giles's voice spiralled upward in disbelief. 'We have to run and hide, like Connall told us. If it's not safe for us to go to Raven's Nest—'

'We have to!' Cordelia's eyes flew open, but she could only glimpse the outlines of her triplets through a thick fog. Mist and flashes of weaponry filled her vision.

And beyond all those …

Raven's Nest.

It was waiting. No, it was *calling* to her, promising every answer she had ever sought about her family, about their past, and about the whole broken kingdom that stretched around her.

They were so close. *Almost there.* The hook in her chest wouldn't let her turn away now. Not for anything.

She could turn into a bird to fly straight there— *no!* She dug in her heels and glared at her triplets' foggy silhouettes.

'We're *all* going there together,' she said stubbornly. 'You *promised*.'

'Argh!' Giles threw up his hands, shifting shadows in her vision. 'How are we supposed to deal with armed soldiers?'

'Well, *you* can probably take care of most of them yourself.' Rosalind's brisk words made both of her triplets turn to stare. She sounded perfectly calm, though, as she continued, 'You've been practising all the way here. Why not just use your sorcery again?'

Giles lurched backwards. 'I ... No, I can't! I *really* can't. Half the time, it won't even work! That first time, I was just so scared, the magic burst out of me.'

'Well, then, *let* yourself feel that scared again.' Rosalind shrugged, swinging her sword-stick in lazy sweeping circles. She bent her legs in preparatory stretches, still holding Cordelia's arm with a firm grip. 'If it doesn't work, they will definitely capture us. Remember that part, and you'll be *more* than scared enough to let your magic free again.'

'But—'

'Look at her!' Rosalind sighed and yanked Cordelia back into place beside her. '*She's* not turning around, no matter what we say. Even if we drag her with us, she'll just turn back and head here on her own the instant we stop holding her. Do *you* want to let her walk into a group of grown soldiers all on her own?'

Giles didn't answer.

Rosalind's voice turned to steel. 'I am not running away like a coward again – and I'm not letting any more of my family be taken prisoner! You can leave us both behind if you like, but I'm staying with Cordy.'

'This is ridiculous!' Giles whisper-shouted …

But Cordelia's shoulders relaxed, because she knew they had won. Giles had never turned away from their family in his life, so – at least for now – they would all keep moving forward together.

18

They all took turns peering over the curve of the final foothill, crouching together behind a massive mossy boulder that would have reached Cordelia's nose if she'd been standing.

The vast slopes of Mount Corve loomed before them, covered in an unbroken dark green treeline. Only faint swirls of white mist curved near its top, but a massive circle of much denser mist surrounded all its lower slopes, ignoring every law of nature.

Soldiers in tunics blazoned with bears and wolves walked along that shimmering shield again and again, pacing an endless, watchful circuit. Like the knights who'd hunted the children in their forest, these ones had abandoned heavy armour for stealth and speed. It must have been obvious to everyone that three unarmed children could present no danger to them.

'I count five.' Rosalind's voice was, for once, a tightly leashed whisper.

'I saw five too.' Giles's fingers jittered against his knees as he rocked anxiously back and forth on the ground, his arms wrapped around his legs.

'There are nine,' Cordelia told them both with utter certainty.

Her vision had finally cleared, as if the land had settled down now it knew she was listening to it once more. But it wasn't the view before her that gave her conviction.

The land was still murmuring into her head, its voices softer now but no less clear and intent.

Giles leaned even closer to peer down at her, his whisper hot against her face. 'How do you *know* these things? What else aren't you telling us?'

'Shh!' Rosalind hissed. 'Save talking for later. All we need to know *now* is there are nine guards waiting. They all know the direction we started out from, but they're not all waiting here together – so there must be more than one way we could be coming.'

'The main road split off a while back,' Giles muttered, rocking in place even faster than before. 'Remember?

Cordy told us which way to go. *Again*.' The look he gave her was narrow-eyed.

'So maybe there's another longer route we could have taken, if we hadn't had Cordy with us as a guide.' Rosalind frowned with concentration. 'We just have to figure out where that one would've come out. Cordy, where are all those other guards waiting right now?'

Cordelia's arm swung left without a thought.

'Got it!' Rosalind smiled fiercely. 'So, *that's* where our voices should be coming from. Go to it!' She clapped Giles on the back.

It sent him rocking into the boulder. '*Careful!*' Clutching his nose, which had taken the brunt of the impact, he glowered at them both. 'Save the bashing for our enemies, Ros. And if Cordy would just trust us, for once—'

'*After the battle*,' Rosalind snapped. 'Now, *go!*'

'*Sisters!*' Giles groaned the word. Then he closed his eyes, drew that familiar deep pre-performance breath …

And Rosalind's voice rang out in the distance, pathetically high-pitched with fear. 'Help! Oh, help me, Giles! I am too afraid to fight!'

The real Rosalind's jaw dropped open in outraged disbelief. Cordelia bit the inside of her cheek to stifle a laugh.

'I'll save you, Ros!' Giles's voice yelled. 'Now that I've got us safely away from all those soldiers who scared you …'

Rosalind snarled soundlessly.

Cordelia's lips tugged into a mischievous grin … until she heard her own voice call out faintly, moving away from the others, 'I don't care what you two do. I'll go my own way, just like always! I don't need anyone else.'

Rosalind gave an appreciative huff.

Cordelia's fingers clenched against the cool, soft moss on the boulder before her. Did Giles actually believe—?

Armed figures shifted in her head. 'They're moving!'

A man's voice bellowed indistinctly in the distance, summoning his comrades to help.

That voice, Cordelia thought, belonged to the Duke of Arden, not to any of the soldiers who were here – but it did the final trick. Inside her head, the line of figures turned, one after another, to run towards their waiting comrades. One, two, three, four in a row …

Oh, no. 'One of them is staying here!'

'Seriously?' As Giles's eyes flew open, the triplets' voices began to fade in the distance.

'Keep going!' Rosalind ordered, rising up on her haunches. 'I'll handle this one.'

'H*ow*? You still don't have a sword!'

'Just remember,' Rosalind murmured as she adjusted the sword-stick in her hand, 'if you let that voice trick of yours stop, I'll have *five* soldiers with real swords to deal with on my own. *Keep going!*'

Giles groaned as he closed his eyes again. Cordelia was too busy making rapid calculations to say anything at all. If she turned into a bear … No – she would get shot by another arrow before she even finished lumbering down the hill. But if she stayed girl *until* she and her sister reached that final soldier, and shifted just before Rosalind could try to swordfight a grown man with that stupid stick …

In one fluid movement, Rosalind leaped to her feet and *threw* the sword-stick. Cordelia jumped up, panic a wild rush within her—

And saw the single remaining soldier crash to the ground, his sword falling uselessly from his hand. Rosalind's heavy sword-stick rebounded and fell on to the grass nearby.

Cordelia gaped at her sister.

Rosalind gave her a ferocious grin. 'You see? H*andled*. You two should finally learn to have faith in me! I keep telling you I'm good.' Reaching down, she yanked their triplet to his feet. 'Now, *run!*'

They ran, skidding and stumbling all the way. The soldier ahead was starting to shake his head as he lay on his back, moaning and feeling for purchase on the ground beside him with his eyes still shut. Rosalind's sword-stick lay on his opposite side. His own long metal sword glinted on the grass by his awkwardly bent legs.

The wall of mist behind him glittered and sparkled in the sun as if it were filled with a million tiny diamonds.

'That is *definitely* not natural,' Giles panted.

'We'll get through it.' Rosalind bared her teeth at the mist ahead as if it were just another enemy waiting to be bashed.

'It'll let us through,' Cordelia promised.

'*Barred against anyone without magic or royal blood* …'

Cordelia might not know exactly whose blood she carried, but every one of the triplets had been born with some kind of magic … and that hook in her chest was reeling her tighter with every breathless moment.

Raven's Nest *wanted* them in its grip.

It was waiting for them.

'Hey!' Between them and the mist, the fallen soldier had opened his eyes. He pushed himself up to his knees, letting out a low grunt of pain. 'Hold!' He clapped one hand to his side, groaning. 'Your Highnesses, *halt immediately!*'

Cordelia veered wide to the left of his big hunched figure.

Ten more feet to go to that sparkling wall of mist …
Eight …

'They're here!' he bellowed, stumbling to his feet. 'Sir
Alina, they're *back here!*'

Footsteps thundered towards them from Cordelia's
other side. Men's and women's voices shouted threats and
commands.

Six more feet …

'This is for your own good!' The soldier scooped his
sword from the grass. 'I can't let you three pass!'

Lunging forward, he grabbed Giles's closest arm with
his free hand.

Giles let out a cry of shock. His arm looked as thin
and breakable as a twig in the man's grip.

Cordelia changed course to run straight at them,
claws and fur readying for battle within her.

'*Leave him alone!*' Rosalind shouted. Her eyes flashed.
She threw her right hand up into the air …

And the big metal sword flew out of the soldier's
hand, knocking him backwards with the force of its
release. Cordelia stopped, gaping.

Rosalind too had finally found a way to make her own
abandoned magic work with her true passion.

Giles twisted free of the soldier's loosened grip as
the sword shot in a high, sweeping curve. Rosalind

caught its pommel neatly in her outstretched hand and then ran forward to shoulder Giles towards the mist. 'Go!'

Their brother ran into the shimmering white wall and disappeared into it. Cordelia couldn't even see his outline through the blinding sparkles.

'Go *now*, Cordy!' Rosalind spun around and dropped into a ready position, swinging her new sword in a wide, threatening curve as soldiers thundered towards them from both directions.

Cordelia hesitated.

'If you've ever loved me, you will *find some faith in me!*' Rosalind gritted.

Nine adult soldiers closed in a shrinking semicircle around her figure.

Cordelia sucked in a frantic breath through her teeth. Then she turned and leaped into the mist.

It closed around her in a chilling full-body embrace. Sparks shot through her veins and exploded through her scalp. Wings and claws and fur and scales all tried to burst out of her skin at once.

Blindly, she stumbled forward through the choking, tingling wet air. White stretched endlessly before her. She couldn't suck in any breath. Her skin burned with cold. Her teeth chattered wildly.

She couldn't even feel her feet any more. Cold prickled at her head, burrowing under her hair as if it were trying to peel her open ... and then dissolve her into the surrounding mist.

She knew that mist. She *recognised* it. It was the same powerful mist that had wrapped around her during Connall's summoning, pulling her back against her will into her own body. It was a power even greater than her own family's magic—

And now, it was trying to take her over completely.

As her head began to swim from lack of air, she shoved her mental walls back into place, using all the skills that she'd been building across her long journey.

I am me, alone. I am Cordelia.

I belong to myself. I will never be trapped again!

The prickles disappeared from her scalp in a rush. The voices of the land emptied out of her head. With a sudden bright burst of energy, she surged forward, and the tips of her fingers poked through into open air.

Long, strong fingers closed around them.

Giles! It had to be.

Thankfully, she allowed herself to be yanked through that final stretch of ancient, magical mist. The moment she broke through into the fresh air of the forest beyond, she fell forward, her head hanging by her knees. Her long hair trailed against the damp mossy ground as she sucked in impossibly noisy breaths. *Free … I'm free!*

The land was whispering against her head again, but she gave a gasping half-laugh of relief as she realised just how muffled those voices had become. Her inner walls were well fortified after her battle through the mist. She couldn't even make out the land's words any more. *Free.*

Cordelia clasped one knee for support with her left hand as she hung on to Giles's surprisingly big hand, just beside her, for the reassurance of his warmth. Before her, just a few feet away, she glimpsed the tips of his familiar pointed shoes, dappled now with shifting shadows from the thick cluster of branches overhead …

And pointing directly towards her.

Wait.

Giles wasn't the one standing beside her after all.

So *who* …?

Dread swept in a cold rush up through her body.

'*Barred against anyone without magic or royal blood* …'

She'd been right: those soldiers couldn't pass through the magical wall of mist. But she and her triplets weren't the only ones who could.

Slowly, painfully, Cordelia rose to her feet. She met Giles's horrified gaze across the aching feet of distance between them, and she swallowed hard. Her brother stood as still as if he'd been frozen, his freckles vivid against his chalk-white face like open wounds. Still not allowing herself to look around, Cordelia gave her right arm a sudden, hard jerk to pull free …

But Lady Elianora's grip on her hand only shifted to clamp tightly around her wrist.

'What a pleasure it is to be reunited with my dear grandchildren.' As Rosalind tumbled through the shimmering wall of mist to land, panting, on her knees by their feet, Lady Elianora's lips curved into a smile of vicious satisfaction. 'This time, I promise you, our little family visit will end *very* differently!'

19

Cordelia shifted in an instant. Fur and muscles and sharp, predatory teeth—

'Ah-ah-ah! I don't think so.' Magic shot through their linked arms in a piercing blast of cold. Gasping, Cordelia landed hard on her knees in her own true form. Lady Elianora shook her head down at her pityingly. Her grip was an iron clamp around Cordelia's wrist. 'You really thought I wouldn't prepare for this encounter, after all that you revealed to me last time?'

'*All that you revealed …*'

A convulsive flinch ran down Cordelia's spine. Her gaze flicked swiftly to Giles – still watching them with panicked blue eyes – and to Rosalind, who was pushing herself heavily to her feet with the long metal sword in her grasp.

Behind them rose the sparkling wall of mist, their only protection against the waiting soldiers. Before them rose the trees that covered Mount Corve, all clothed in a mysterious and primeval dark green, their ancient trunks knotted and looming. No birds called in those powerful twisted branches, but Cordelia could feel hidden eyes fixed upon her and her family, silently watching their human catastrophe unfold in the shadowed, murky mountain air.

'Oh, but how *interesting*,' Lady Elianora murmured. 'I find myself wondering: have you actually shared with your – *siblings* – all that you learned from me?'

'Step away from our sister, Grandmother.' Rosalind was still flushed and panting from her own trip through the mist, but she raised the heavy sword in a practised move and aimed it steadily at Lady Elianora. 'Let Cordy go.'

'So she really hasn't told you!' Lady Elianora tipped her head back with a billowing laugh, her long nails digging sharply into Cordelia's wrist. 'Oh, this is delightful. All the best family secrets can come out to play!'

'What are you talking about?' Giles's face was pale and haunted in the shadows of the knobbly tree branches that arched over them all, twisting and tangling together into a cage. 'Cordy? What's going on?'

Numbly, Cordelia shook her head. I *was supposed to have more time!*

Power, deep and ancient, thrummed against her knees from the cool, damp ground beneath the thin fabric of her dirty dress. Tiny leftover scraps of mist crept and curled across the dark moss around her.

Old magic.

The tug of the hook in her chest was a dull, persistent throb. They were *so close* to Raven's Nest. If only she had been faster! If only she hadn't had to stop so often to rest!

'One more chance, Grandmother.' Rosalind held her sword steady. 'Let Cordy go, or else.'

'Or else … *what*, dear?' Lady Elianora raised one eyebrow enquiringly, her tone gentle. 'Are you really going to attack your own grandmother?'

Rosalind swallowed visibly, but her sword didn't waver. 'You attacked us, before. Cordy told us.'

'And you still trust her to tell you the whole truth?' Lady Elianora clucked disapprovingly.

Rosalind traded a quick startled glance with Giles.

'That's what *happened!*' Cordelia found her voice at last. 'You can't pretend you didn't put us all to sleep and pile us into that awful chest.'

'It was a *cedar* chest, actually, and a very fine one too. It's not as if I had any guest beds to spare in that pathetic little hut, did I?' Lady Elianora's nostrils flared with distaste. '*Your* mother's treacherous misbehaviour saw *me* expelled from court with all my greatest treasures confiscated. That chest was by far the most comfortable resting place that I could have given any of you! And yet –' her eyes narrowed – '*you* didn't stay inside, did you, dear? You somehow woke up and escaped – *only* you. Haven't Rosalind and Giles found themselves wondering how that could have been?'

'It was because I didn't trust you.' Cordelia gritted the words through clenched teeth. 'Connall *told* me that was why the spell couldn't hold me as long as it held the others.'

'Oh, yes, you were remarkably untrusting from the beginning – which was *quite* unlike the others. I noticed how different you were straight away. I'd guess that they must have seen it too by now. Haven't you, my dears?' Lady Elianora tilted her head, her voice confiding. 'Surely there's been something just a bit … *off* … about your unfortunate sister from the very beginning. Little hints you might not have even let yourself understand, like—'

'Enough!' growled Rosalind. 'We won't stand here and listen to you insult our sister.'

Cordelia let out a shuddering breath of relief …

'No.' The word fell from Giles's lips like a heavy stone into the shadowy space between them. 'I want to hear Cordy tell us the truth herself – and I'm not waiting any longer.'

Cordelia couldn't remember a single day of her existence when she hadn't looked into Giles's dreamy blue eyes and known – no matter how much they might bicker along the way – that she was absolutely accepted by him.

Now, her sweet, impractical triplet brother looked at her as if she were a dangerous stranger ... and he took a step away from her. 'I want to trust you with the truth,' he said quietly, 'but Grandmother's right. I can't.'

'Giles?' Rosalind frowned, her sword lowering. 'What are you doing?'

Between them, Lady Elianora didn't say a word ... but Cordelia could actually *feel* her smile.

Giles aimed his words at Rosalind, his gaze averted from Cordelia's face. 'It just hit me, at last, while we were waiting to get through the mist. Don't you remember how Cordy led us through our forest back home? *She* knew the way out even though she'd never seen it. She told us *exactly* how close those knights were getting ... just like she told us where these soldiers were before we could step into their trap.'

Cordelia swallowed, waiting. Lady Elianora hummed a quietly satisfied note of encouragement.

Rosalind frowned at Giles. 'So?'

'There was no way for her to know any of that! But she wouldn't explain to us how she did it, and there was no *reason* for her to keep it secret ... unless ...' He took a deep breath. 'All this time, I thought she was only upset by something Grandmother said. I *trusted* that she wouldn't keep anything important from us.

'But that wouldn't explain everything else that she's managed from the very beginning of this ... until it finally occurred to me: What if she's been talking to someone else all along?'

Cordelia blinked.

Rosalind said, 'Who—?'

'Just think about it, Ros!' His rigid expression shattered; his next words were a cry of pain. 'We only know two people who could do that – who would even *want* to do it in the first place. Who else could it be?' He shook his head, his flushed cheeks hollowing. 'I should have figured it out – I even wondered, once or twice – but I couldn't *believe* she would keep the two of them secret from us. Not until now.' He let out a bitter laugh. 'Cordy doesn't care to share any of her secrets with us any more, does she?'

'Giles ...' Cordelia began in a pained whisper.

But Lady Elianora's voice was louder. 'Clever boy,' she purred. 'You can see now how she's been tricking you all along, can't you? The truth is, I'm the *only* one you two can trust any more. That's why she dragged you away from me before, without even giving me the chance to defend myself against her wild claims.'

Giles didn't respond to her words – but his jaw hardened as he looked at Cordelia, his blue eyes fierce with pain and anger. 'I don't think you only talked to Connall once, after all. I think you've been talking either to him or to Mother all along – and lying to us about it every step of the way.'

'Don't be an idiot!' Cordelia shoved herself to her feet, Lady Elianora's grip an iron manacle around her wrist. 'You know I wouldn't do that!'

'Do we? Really?' The tip of Rosalind's sword finally lowered to the ground as she stared at Cordelia, breathing hard. 'If you've been talking to them all this time without telling us, when you *knew* how scared for them we've been …'

'Well, of course she has,' said Lady Elianora. 'Can't you see it? Keeping secrets from you two is what she does best.'

'Don't listen to her!' Cordelia cried. 'Giles! Ros! You *know* me. You know I wouldn't—'

'Then how could you tell that those soldiers were waiting by the mist?' Giles demanded. 'How did that arrow wound of yours heal in only an hour? And do you really think I'm so stupid, I haven't *noticed* there's been magic at work every night while Ros and I were sleeping? I've seen those flowers underneath you every morning! Are *they* part of the magic that lets you talk to Connall and Mother without either of us listening in?'

'*No!*' Cordelia yelled. 'Mother and Connall didn't heal me. I can't reach out to them any more than you can. I would have told you if I could. Trust me!'

'*Trust* you to tell us anything? You haven't trusted *us* for days!' Hissing out a breath, Rosalind threw up her hands, letting her sword fall to the ground. 'How stupid do you think we are?'

'If you're stupid enough to think I would *ever*—'

'Enough!' Giles's cry rang out through the shadowy green air. Unshed tears shimmered in his eyes. 'I am *finished* trusting you when you refuse to trust us back. Cordy, if you can't tell us the whole truth, *right now*, then we're not coming any further with you. Not one more step!'

Rosalind's jaw clenched visibly with tension … but she gave a short, sharp nod of agreement.

Cordelia's whole body shook as if it were tearing itself apart … or trying to pull her back in time, to change that first terrible night for good, to keep them all safely planted within the walls of their castle, with every terrifying secret kept walled outside forever. 'If I tell you the truth, I'll lose you anyway!' Her words fell into the air like broken pieces.

'Cordy?' Giles's voice softened as he started forward. 'What are you talking about? You're our sister. As long as you're honest with us, there's nothing you could ever say that—'

'Oh, but she's not actually your sister. That's what she's been too cowardly to tell you!' Lady Elianora's voice rang with satisfaction as she swept forward to stand between them. 'She never belonged in your little family in the first place. I could tell at a glance that she was wilder and far less suited to the throne than either of you dear children – and there certainly were not three infants in your mother's belly when she fled into that nightmarish forest!'

Lady Elianora beamed fiercely down at Rosalind and Giles's stunned faces. 'My dears, I am so terribly sorry you've had to suffer this awful shock. As the only true family you have left now, I hope you'll give me the chance to prove my good intentions. Just come with me and—'

'No!' Cordelia yelped. 'Giles – Ros – even if you leave me, please don't trust her. She'll—'

'Wait.' Giles stared up at Lady Elianora. 'You told Cordy she wasn't our real sister? Just because she … was adopted when she was a baby? Or something like that?'

'Well, of course she's our sister,' Rosalind said flatly. 'Don't be absurd! If that's what you've been holding over Cordy's head that's made her turn so grumpy and ridiculous …' In one smooth move, Rosalind scooped her sword up and pointed it directly at her grandmother. 'We'll stay right here with her, thank you, and you can leave without *all* of us.'

'I'll explain all the tedious details to you later, my dears.' Lady Elianora's voice sharpened with irritation. 'It all comes down to your mother's deceptions, as usual. But you two and I have fabulous places to go now and some very important people to meet. So I'm afraid that I simply must insist …'

She held out her free hand. Magic gathered thickly in the air with an all-too-familiar prickling against Cordelia's skin.

Cordelia couldn't transform to protect her triplets while their grandmother gripped her wrist. She had no sorcery of her own to change the world around her, either. But Connall had said there was a key to unlocking every spell – and a power far greater than her own family's magic thrummed through the earth beneath her.

Some things were even more important than freedom.

'You will *never* take my family away from me!' she snarled.

Then she dropped every one of her inner walls of protection to speak directly to the land. *I'm here. I'm ready.*

Just save Giles and Rosalind, and – I promise – I'll do whatever it is you've wanted from me all along!

Magic coiled through the air around Lady Elianora as she spun around to face Cordelia, flinging out her free hand.

Earth erupted directly beneath her. She staggered back, fingers finally loosening around Cordelia's wrist.

Cordelia yanked herself free and stumbled back, gasping and rubbing at her bruised skin … and was caught in a chilling, all-enveloping embrace.

White mist surged from the magical shield behind her to scoop all three children safely from the ground just as a deep and narrow chasm suddenly opened beneath their feet. Lady Elianora's voice rose in a cry of shock. For one impossibly long moment, Cordelia watched her teeter on the chasm's edge, arms pinwheeling wildly through the mist.

Then the ground beneath Lady Elianora gave one last, impatient surge. It shoved her forward, into mid-air, and she fell into the endless darkness, shrieking with furious despair.

Dirt sealed shut above her outstretched fingertips. Grass cut off her distant cries.

All three children had been left untouched by the sudden, violent breach …

But Cordelia and her triplets were all moving by then too, still embraced by the mist and shooting up the mountainside at a terrifying breakneck pace.

Knotted branches blurred past them on all sides, as faint and untouchable as ghosts. Cordelia twisted desperately within the thick, damp white air, flailing with both hands to find her triplets. All she could see were their hazy silhouettes. Finally, *finally*, their hands closed around hers and held on tight ...

But she lost sight even of their dim outlines as they neared the top of the mountain and the hook inside her chest found its anchor at last.

At last.

We have you.

We've been waiting for so long!

Ancient, inhuman voices boomed around her, deafening her.

Visions swarmed in upon all her senses.

... And Cordelia lost herself entirely to the spirits of Raven's Nest.

20

S he saw it all …

Ravens. Badgers. Bears. Wolves. Rabbits. Falcons. All the *green, growing things, all filled with spirit. All the different patchwork pieces of the land fitting together in perfect harmony.*

Then humans. Wars.

Spirits rising from the earth, taking shape in the land's defence.

Bloodshed. Battles. Disharmony everywhere …

Finally, a hard-won agreement among all.

The spirits — those powerful few that survived — retreating to Raven's Nest, the centre of their strength. Their magic spreading throughout the land, keeping borders strong and human rulers safe. Rulers' connection to the land keeping harvests thriving and weather kind.

In return, human sorcerers working with the spirits to forge the Raven Crown on the slopes of Mount Corve. Both sides blending their greatest magics. Each side making true sacrifices to seal the great promise, to be held fast for all their sakes:

Harmony. Unity. Peace.

For everyone.

Heart and spirit and fierce protection combining in perfect unison for centuries, binding land and people together …

Until human rulers forget the ancient promises forged into their magical crown. All they see is the power that it carries – and the opportunities for more. They turn against the land that they've sworn to protect. They break the old contracts for the sake of their greed.

The crown breaks with them into three pieces. No human magic can ever repair it.

Sister turns on brother, cousin on cousin. Forests burn to ashes. Blood spills across the broken landscape.

No more unity. No harmony between people and land anywhere.

Until …

A dark-haired, round-bellied sorceress creeps through the night, holding tightly to the hands of one tight-lipped friend and one small, frightened boy with shadows in his eyes.

The sorceress wraps strong spells of protection around the wild forest that she enters, holding it safe from all the battles outside. The forest folds her into its own heart in gratitude. When her babe is born and the forest hears those rare, raw tears that she weeps for her child's future – and overhears her final, desperate plan to hide her newborn child – then, the forest chooses to help her in return, stirred by more reasons than it can fathom for itself.

For once, all the different, fractured pieces of the land are working in unison again.

Two creatures for the spell, they send: a newborn hare and a fox cub, who both pad into the sorceress's keeping exactly when she needs them. The whole land pours its green magic into her spell as she casts it – and what a spell it becomes!

With human or land magic alone, it would have been impossible. Working together, something miraculous takes place. An act of transformation: two new babes, to hide the third one in plain sight.

She'd only wanted the three babes tied together for her own babe's protection, to hide her true child from any seeking eyes.

But every spirit of the land feels the click of true connection when it forms. It knows that the moment they've awaited for decades has arrived at long last.

Humanity and wildness, heart and spirit and fierce protection, all tie together once more in a bond that must never be broken.

Raven's Nest still carries the memory of that final moment

as it rippled through every piece of the broken kingdom, filling it with the wildest, most desperate hope and joy.

Three human infants lie together on a white cot by the castle window, snuggled into each other: three parts of a perfect whole. Even their soft breaths are shared.

The same size. The same skin. So nearly interchangeable.

'No one can ever know the truth.' The sorceress's low voice carries through the open window to the listening, watching forest outside. 'We can't even tell Connall. He's been through so much already. He's too young to bear such heavy secrets. If we ever have to run as a family, we'll tell him – but not until then.'

'Do you really think it can be so simple?' The other woman sighs and shakes her head. 'They may have started as something else, Kathryn, but they're children now. Your children. Can you truly give up the others to protect her, once you've raised them all as your own?'

'What choice do I have?' The sorceress straightens until she is out of sight from the window, but her voice cuts like a dagger through the night air. 'I couldn't keep Connall safe, and he isn't even a royal heir. I will protect Cordelia no matter what sacrifices I have to make. That bloodthirsty throne won't steal her from me too!'

At the rage in her rising voice, all three infants stir restlessly – first one and then the others, all twisting and whimpering together.

Leaning over the cot, she lets out a long breath. Then she strokes her long fingers across all three chests in a row and begins to sing the low, familiar tune that the forest heard her humming all through her pregnancy:

'Little ones, go to sleep; it is time now for dreaming ...'

The forest sighs its appreciation of the lilting, comforting tune. It lets itself finally sleep too, to the sound of that lullaby. It has been drained of its power for the moment, but it is content to rest and wait while that new green shoot grows to save all of them.

White clouds of mist snapped apart, leaving Cordelia reeling. Her breath was a burning bellows in her chest. Panting, she blinked and blinked again ...

And found both of her triplets standing with her on the high slopes of Mount Corve, with all her own horror reflected in their faces.

The past and the present blurred in all their eyes ...

And a broken silver crown, engraved with starflowers, lay in three pieces on the grass between them.

21

Giles moistened his lips with his tongue and swallowed, his face bone-white. 'No wonder,' he whispered, 'you didn't want to tell us. You really were trying to protect us.' His lips stretched into a painfully false smile. 'I'm sorry I didn't trust you, Cor—Your Majesty. I'll just—'

'No!' Even Cordelia was startled by the force of her own panicked bellow.

It was too much. *Everything* was too much. She'd spent her life trying to find out her family's deepest secrets, but none of the pieces of the past made any sense as they whirled around her now. The unmistakable feeling of her brother's retreat was enough to tear away her last anchor.

'It's not right,' she said. 'It *can't* be right! I'm not the Raven Heir.'

Even Lady Elianora hadn't believed that. *She'd* been more than ready to put Giles or Rosalind on the throne.

No one would ever want to offer Cordelia a crown ... least of all herself.

'But you are. Of course you are!' Giles's lips twisted. 'How could I not have seen it before? You weren't talking to Mother or Connall after all. You've been talking to the land all along, haven't you? *That's* how you knew what was happening in our forest – and it was the land that healed you too.'

'So maybe I was the one who started out as an animal! That's what you two always called me, remember? *Everyone* knows I'm wild and feral. I'm just—'

'You're tied to the land. You always have been.' Rosalind shook her head slowly, her eyes shuttered and impossible to read. 'That's why Mother –' she bit her lip, then forged onwards – 'I mean, why the *Duchess* could never keep you inside our castle. The land was calling to you all along ... Your Majesty.'

Lowering her head, Rosalind dropped heavily to one knee on the grass and placed her sword before her in submission.

'No!' Half sobbing, Cordelia lunged forward to drag her sister upright. '*Don't do that!*'

'Why not?' Giles's tone was terrifyingly empty. 'We're only your loyal subjects. What else can we be?'

She could *see* him preparing to turn and walk away. She knew him. She knew them both to her very core.

How could she ever have doubted their true relationship?

'Lady Elianora told me I wasn't your real sister,' she said, 'but I should have known better than to believe her. She's never understood what family means! You were right before when you told her it doesn't matter how we first came together. *Our father* told Connall the same thing – and I should have understood it from the beginning. Real family is about love and loyalty, not blood!'

'But why didn't Grandm—I mean, *Lady Elianora* tell us Mother was only carrying one child when she first ran to the woods?' Rosalind tugged free of Cordelia's grip to clutch her sword with both hands. 'If she could tell that Mother wasn't really carrying triplets, couldn't she tell there was only one baby, not two?'

'I know the answer to that question.' Giles's voice was dry and bitter. 'She said it herself, didn't she, Ros? You and I were the ones who were foolish enough to trust her. Cordy sensed the truth from the beginning – so Lady Elianora knew the two of us would be easier for her to manage once she got one of us on to the throne. *She* didn't care which of us was her real grandchild.'

'She said she knew Mother's magic as well as her own.' Cordelia's chest twisted at the unhidden pain on her brother's face. 'When she saw all three of us together, she must have guessed that Mother had cast a spell like that as a ruse.'

'But then why didn't Mother – the Duchess – bother to *use* it?' A fierce sob choked Rosalind's voice. 'If she was never really our mother all along – if she only brought in me and Giles to give you cover whenever the soldiers finally made it past all her spells ... then why wouldn't she let me fight by her side, in the end? Why would she even care whether I was hurt?'

'Maybe she had another plan by then. Nothing else had changed, had it?' Giles's lips curved in an unhappy twist. 'We were still the two spares that she planned to give up to keep her real child safe.' He exchanged a long look with Rosalind over Cordelia's shoulder. 'If *real family* is about love and loyalty ... then I think we all know where we stand now. Don't we?'

Panic spiralled in Cordelia's gut.

She could lose them both right now. She could *feel* the connection that had held her steady all her life just waiting to snap.

'She didn't give you up, though. She told *all of us* to run. She said that she loved us *all*.' Cordelia fixed her gaze on Giles's ashen face, willing him to listen. 'There *has* to be more to it than we saw.'

He shook his head, looking unbearably weary. 'Who knows? We can't ask her about any of it now – and she never answered any of our questions anyway. But we all heard what she said in the beginning, and there's nothing that you can say now to change it.'

He was right: words had never been Cordelia's speciality. Those belonged to Giles, as fighting did to Rosalind. All that Cordelia had was her own inherent wildness. Her connection to the land.

… The connection that the other two had gifted her when their spirits had fused with hers. *That* was why the magic she'd inherited from Mother hadn't turned into ordinary sorcery, as it had for all her siblings. Instead, it had fused with the first natures of her triplets. She'd given her inherited human sorcery to them, and they'd shaped her nature in return, giving her the gift of their wildness.

They were just like the pieces of the broken land itself. Each of them held their own singular powers, but they would always be strongest when they worked together.

Desperation gave her strength. She grabbed their hands and refused to let go when they both tried to pull away.

'Make a circle,' she snapped. 'All in one. *Exactly* like those first founding magics wanted.'

She'd told them earlier that she couldn't reach out to Mother. It had been the truth, as far as she had known at that point. She *didn't* have the power to cast summonings, not like Connall.

But she had let the land in now. She had accepted its claim.

Together, she and her triplets formed all three parts of the triad that it needed.

Heart – that was Giles, and it always had been: the open, overflowing heart of the whole family, breaking now before her eyes. *She had to fix it.*

Protection? That part could never be in any doubt. Rosalind set down her sword reluctantly to take Giles's free hand in hers. She squared her broad shoulders in visible preparation for any battle ahead.

Spirit … Cordelia took a breath and flung herself wide open.

Power rocked through her like the wildest of storms. She squeezed her eyes shut and gripped her triplets' hands hard to stay upright on the rough mountain path as ancient green magic filled her to overflowing.

Overwhelming. Terrifying. Incredible. The feeling made

her head spin and her body shake like a tree caught in high winds.

We're all here, she told the land. *I'm yours, just as you wanted. Now show her to us! I know you can.*

Giles's hand tightened around hers as Cordelia shook with the power that raged through her body, like a willow tree whipped back and forth by a storm. Rosalind let out a harsh breath and shoved one strong, bracing shoulder against Cordelia's side to keep her from toppling.

Green and blue snapped into place and filled Cordelia's vision as her mind's eye hurtled through the miles. *Blue sky ahead and a green landscape below.*

That landscape moved faster and faster, blurring with speed as all three children flew high above it. They passed sprawling army camps, hopelessly burning fields, and groups of refugees streaming down the long roads. Finally, in her mind's eye, they swooped over a set of strong stone walls into a dirty, crowded city with a sprawling castle at its centre. Bear and wolf flags flew from its ramparts. Armed guards marched threateningly along its square towers – but none of them seemed to glimpse any of the three children who soared through the air towards them.

Cordelia's feet were still planted on Mount Corve. She felt her triplets' solid hands in hers, anchoring her as always. But behind her closed eyelids, she was swept through the air, and Giles and Rosalind flew invisibly beside her until they finally came to a halt, peering down together through the high tower window where the land had brought them.

It was a tiny arched opening without any glass, laced with brutal iron bars. It looked down into a suffocatingly small rectangular room, where a familiar figure paced the stone floor like a wild animal trapped inside a cage.

Mother's hair must have fallen out of its plait long ago. It whirled around her now in a wild, tangled cloud as she spun to stare upward with bloodshot dark eyes. 'Who's watching me this time?' she snapped. 'Mother? Is that you again? I've told you, your tricks don't work on me any more.'

A spark of gold glinted around her neck, half hidden beneath her hair. Mother had never worn necklaces before. Why would her captors give her jewellery?

That isn't jewellery. Cordelia sucked in her breath, squeezing down hard on her triplets' hands. That was a *collar* pinching tightly around Mother's neck – the collar that Connall had mentioned in his summoning.

Air hissed furiously through Rosalind's teeth.

'So *that's* how they stopped her reaching out to us.' Giles's voice was low and sad.

Cordelia could sense it too: the sickly burning pulse of that tight collar as it held Mother's magic trapped, helpless within her body. No wonder she looked so drawn and sick.

It was more than wrong to see Mother without her power. It was *wicked*.

But that collar couldn't keep her body still. Mother lunged forward, eyes widening and hands flying up to clench the stone wall below the window. 'Giles? Is that you?' she asked hoarsely.

For once, Giles didn't utter a single word. Cordelia couldn't see him in her vision, but she could hear him – and his quick breaths sounded jagged. *Broken.*

She said as steadily as she could, 'It's all of us. And, Mother …' She took a deep, steadying breath. 'We know.'

'Cordelia?' Mother's eyes narrowed as she rose on tiptoes to reach higher towards the barred window, still hopelessly far out of her reach. 'What are you talking about?'

'We know why you never answered any of our questions about the past,' Cordelia said quietly. 'We saw it all: how Giles and Rosalind first came to us … and what you planned to do to them.'

Mother's jaw dropped open. She stumbled backwards, her hands falling to her sides. 'Cordelia, I … Children …'

Head bowing, she reached out one trembling hand to balance herself against the curving stone wall. Mother had always been a pillar of strength – fierce and sure and infuriatingly immovable. Now, she looked years older and suddenly horribly uncertain.

'Have you even been eating?' Giles's voice shook on the words. 'Or have they been starving you in there?'

Mother *was* thinner than she had been, Cordelia realised. It was part of what made her look so frail and breakable.

She shook her head without looking up. 'I've eaten,' she said dully. 'I have to make myself eat to stay strong.'

'Strong for *what*?' There were tears choking Rosalind's voice now. 'You're a prisoner. They've trapped your magic. What can you do any more?'

'What do you think?' Mother's head swung up, her gaze ferocious even as tears sparkled like fallen stars in her dark eyes. 'I have to stay strong so I can escape and find all of you! I *need* to get free to protect you.'

'You mean you need to protect *Connall and Cordelia*,' Giles muttered.

'Giles!' Impatience rang in her voice as she dashed one dirty hand over her eyes. 'Don't be ridiculous.'

'I'm just telling the truth!' Of all the triplets, Giles had always had the easiest relationship with their mother. He'd never entered into any of the blazing rows that had flared between her and Cordelia; never complained as Rosalind had whenever she couldn't get the weapons that she'd wanted for her training. Now, Cordelia heard true heartbreak in the unfamiliar rage that suffused his voice. 'You don't need to pretend any more. Ros and I *know* that we're not your real children. You never cared about us at all.'

'Don't you dare say that!' Mother straightened away from the wall, eyes flashing. 'That's a lie, and you know it.'

'We heard you say it,' Giles said, 'in Cordy's vision.'

'We saw *and* we heard,' Rosalind added.

'Wait,' Cordelia breathed. '*Wait*.' They *had* all heard what Mother had said. But … 'We heard what Alys said too. Remember? She said it didn't matter how you two started: that you were Mother's children from then onwards. Just as Connall was Father's too.'

How could it possibly be any different? All three triplets had slept curled together from the first night she'd been born. They'd shared the same air. They'd grown in each other's light.

They were family in every possible way.

'Well, *your* mother said that that couldn't matter,' Giles snarled back at Cordelia. 'She said she'd have to sacrifice the two of us anyway.'

'I *was wrong!*'

Mother's words were so unexpected that all three of them fell silent in pure shock.

Mother *never* admitted to any mistakes. She never gave up on any argument, no matter how small.

Now she said bitterly, 'I was a fool. Alys knew better from the very beginning. She let me do what I had to when I was mad with grief and fear, but she understood the truth even before I did.' She shook her head, face drawn and haggard. 'I think you – all of you – were less than a week old when I realised exactly what an idiot I'd been. To nurse a child with my own milk – rock them to sleep in my arms – and then leave them to their death?'

She shook her head sharply in dismissal. 'I would have cut off my own limbs before I let *any* of you be hurt, even back then, when I scarcely knew you. Now that I've raised you –' she gave a harsh, broken laugh – 'have I *ever* given you any reason to believe I cared less about any of you? All four of you, with Connall, are my *heart*. You are my reason for everything I do! I could *never* sacrifice any of my children, no matter what the cause.'

'But your mother could,' Cordelia said. 'Couldn't she?'

Their mother's face tightened. Her words ground out through clenched teeth. 'My mother knows nothing of family. I only learned what it meant when Connall was born – and your father taught me the rest when he embraced Connall as his own. I fled to the forest instead of staying to fight because I wouldn't let my *true* family be twisted as my first family had been. As *so many* families have been twisted by that blood-soaked throne over the years! Everything that I've done since then has been designed to keep all four of my children safe. That's why I never told any of you the truth. How could I bear to hurt any of you like that?'

So many families … Cordelia thought of Alys and the bear-duke brother who had cast her off so completely. 'I *have no sister* …'

As long as the Raven Crown stayed broken, more and more families would tear themselves apart through their terrible battles for the throne … and the land would break more and more grievously every time.

'*No one* is going to hurt any more of my children,' said their mother fiercely. 'I'd happily give up anything to keep you all safe. I'd do anything to free Connall. I'd be a prisoner for all my life if it would help! Just *stay together* now, *please*. Protect each other! And run as far as possible from that terrible throne. Even if you can never forgive me, at least promise me that you'll do that.'

'I … Oh, you know we love you too, Mother.' Giles's voice was muffled with tears. He sniffed hard, forcing them back. 'You should have told us everything. You should have trusted us to understand! I'm going to be angry at you for a really long time about that. But … we do love you too. Of course we do.'

Rosalind gave a choked snort of agreement.

Cordelia said firmly, 'We *all* love you. But we still won't make that promise.'

'What?' Their mother stared wildly around the air, following the sound of Cordelia's voice and grabbing out, uselessly, with one hand. 'Cordelia, don't you *dare* consider even for a single *instant*—'

The vision vanished with a snap as Cordelia let it go.

'Real families don't abandon each other,' she told her stunned-looking, tear-streaked triplets on the shadowy slope of Mount Corve, where the deepest and most dangerous secrets had finally come out into the light, 'and our family hasn't broken after all.' She squeezed their hands tightly in hers. 'So it's time to save the others and make things right. *Together*.'

22

On her own, Cordelia would have had to beg the land to lead her, listening for directions with every step she took. Having her triplets by her side made everything so much easier. While she had trotted in horse form across the kingdom, keeping her focus on the mountains, and Rosalind had stayed alert to human threats, Giles had apparently drawn maps in his head and taken amazingly detailed mental notes of everything they'd passed.

'I recognised the city where Mother's being held,' he told them as they walked back down Mount Corve, ducking under twisted overhanging branches and avoiding brambles. 'It's only two days from here, but that army wasn't camped outside the walls when we passed it two days ago.'

Rosalind scowled consideringly as she pushed another branch out of her way. 'Those flags in the army camp around it – they were boars, badgers and falcons, weren't they? So, the Duchess of Solenne and her allies are gathered there, trying to take the city for their own heir.'

'Yet another battle waiting to happen,' Cordelia said wearily. Inside her head, various pieces were moving through the near distance – the land keeping her aware of the positions of all nine soldiers still waiting outside the mist. *They* would be easy to slip past now that she'd welcomed the land's guidance – but whole armies would be far trickier to avoid.

Rosalind nodded firmly. 'The Dukes of Lune and Arden must be holding the castle with Mother and Alys and Connall as their prisoners. Without the three of us, though, they can't claim the Raven Throne – because everyone agrees that *they* aren't the next heirs.'

'Who's most likely to win that siege?' Giles asked.

'Who knows?' Rosalind shrugged. 'All *we* need to know is that our family is trapped inside … and this time, we're not running away from the battle.'

They didn't. They aimed towards it instead once they slipped back through the mist. Cordelia became a sleek black horse once more, with a new makeshift sack hanging around her neck, while Rosalind and Giles rode together on her back. This time, though, every time they stopped to rest, she shifted immediately into girl form so that they could talk through all their memories and fears, trying to fill in the gaps in the history of their family.

Those gaps were still wide open and hurting. Giles hadn't sung even once since they had left Mount Corve. He kept starting to, then stopping himself with a wince, shrinking inward as if some vital flame had faded to a bare flicker within him.

Rosalind seemed to have shrunk as well. She might have found her own way back to sorcery outside Mount Corve, but now, whenever their conversations died down and her practice sessions came to an end, she sat with her shoulders hunched and her expression dour.

Still, they were both staying with Cordelia, surrounding her – *including* her – and she needed them now more badly than she ever had before … because there was no closing off the land around her any more. Every one of her internal barriers had been ripped away for good on the slopes of Mount Corve. Now, every step she took, whether by hoof or by foot, cast echoes ringing through her ears as a thousand voices cried into her head at once.

Broken! Broken! Broken! Heal us!

I'll try, she promised them, again and again.

She still didn't know how to heal the crown itself. None of them could work it out, no matter how many times they'd argued over different possibilities or even tried to press the pieces together with their hands – but she'd carried it with her in that sack anyway. Their long trip, along with her visions on Mount Corve, had taught her something that she could never forget: her family wasn't all that needed saving.

Still, if her triplets hadn't clustered around her non-stop, asking her endless questions and demanding her responses – if she hadn't had their constant reminders of who she, *Cordelia*, was at her core – her own stubborn internal voice would have been drowned out by the end of the first day.

She'd spent all her life desperate to escape the confining walls of Mother's castle and plunge into the wild forest and world outside. According to her triplets' new theories, the land had probably been calling to her all along – and it had finally managed to make real contact when she'd fallen asleep on the grass after her arrow wound. That had been the first time in her life that she had slept outside in her own true form, leaving herself entirely unshielded.

Now, whenever she closed her eyes at night, lying on hard ground, she could reach out with her senses and *feel* all the miles around her as if they stretched out from her own skin, pulling her body taut … and plunging her mind deep into the awareness of the earth that cradled all of them.

Humans moved across the ground in groups; one horrifyingly large, loud group busily burned and tore at the soil as the land shrieked in agony. Its attackers clanked with metal armour as they slashed down ancient trees, and the land cried endlessly to the only pair of ears that heard it:

Broken. Broken. Broken. Heal—

'Cordy!' Giles leaned over her, frowning as her eyes flew open. 'Didn't you hear us calling you?'

'Sorry.' She took a deep breath and pushed herself up. Dawn had broken over the nearby farmland. Rosalind – several feet away – looked as if she was finally nearing the end of her usual morning exercises, which had been increased to include new, magical elements ever since her battle at Mount Corve. 'Just give me a minute and I'll be ready.'

'We're not far now.' Giles was still frowning down at her. 'Maybe I shouldn't have woken you up. If you really need more sleep—'

'I wasn't sleeping.' Cordelia hadn't truly slept since they'd left Raven's Nest. She'd only drifted as the land had dragged her under every night. Even her triplets couldn't manage to distract her from that while they slept.

'If you say so,' he said, 'but you *looked*—'

'I was listening.' She climbed wearily to her feet. 'There are a *lot* of people moving around right now between us and the closest city.'

'Well, that'll be the army we saw before.' His frown deepened. 'Cordy ...'

'Everyone ready?' Rosalind's face was red from exertion, and her short thick hair stood away from her face in wild sweaty hanks, but she grinned fiercely as she strode towards them, dusting her hands against her sides. Her sheathed sword hung ready at her hip, slapping briskly against her leg with every step. '*Finally*. Today's the day we fight!'

'Don't get too carried away,' Giles said. 'Remember, you're not taking on that whole army by yourself.'

She shrugged, her spine so tight it looked ready to snap. 'I wouldn't need to take on the whole army. If I could figure out which ones are the dukes and duchesses—'

'Rosalind!' He ground the heels of both hands into his forehead. 'Just *follow the plan*. First, we try to find a way to sneak past them all without being noticed. Then, *if* that works, we find Mother and Connall, get Mother's collar off her neck, and then *they'll* take care of any fighting that's needed. Got it?'

'Ha.' She tilted her head at Cordelia. 'Have you told *her* that?'

'Cordy isn't the one who wants to go charging at hundreds of grown men with swords!'

'Of course not,' Rosalind said. 'She has me to do that for her. Find some faith!'

Giles looked between the two of them and groaned piteously. 'Just … *try* to stay quiet,' he begged. 'We might still manage to sneak into the city without being noticed. It *could* happen.'

Rosalind rolled her eyes at Cordelia … who nodded in silent agreement.

She *had* tried to tell Giles how many soldiers she had sensed between them and those high city walls. Even she wasn't prepared for the sight that greeted them when they finally arrived, though. From the hilltop where they stopped to stare, it looked as if the whole valley ahead had turned into a shifting quilt of martial colours, with barely a speck of grass left to be seen.

Boars, badgers and falcons flew high on rippling flags around the strong stone walls. Hundreds of armed men and women in red and brown padded tunics surrounded every inch of stone and swept out around them in a wide circle of threat. Even if they had been the only obstacles, there would have been no *sneaking past without being noticed* for the triplets.

But even more soldiers had arrived since the day of their shared vision – and these ones carried the competing wolf and bear flags of the Dukes of Lune and Arden. They had camped in a wider circle around the group of besiegers, hemming them in.

Between the two camps, two smaller groups stood facing each other in the middle of the field underneath a white flag, looking angrier and angrier with every sweeping gesture.

Sharp weapons bristled in every direction.

But it wasn't Cordelia's own fear that hit her like a tidal wave as she gazed down at the battlefield. It was a fear passed on to her by the land, and it originated beyond those high city walls – walls that could never withstand a battle of this size.

There were thousands of people crammed inside that city. They might have fled behind those walls for protection, but now there was no way for any of them to escape. Cordelia's heightened senses marked out every adult and child's body currently packed into that suffocatingly constricted space, all huddled around each other in desperation ... thousands of living, breathing human bodies that were about to become yet more broken pawns in the dukes and duchesses' endless wars for power.

Cordelia's senses were tied into the land on which those people huddled, not into the people themselves. But their panic and terror was so intense, the emotions bled into the ground of the city like an infection, and the land fed every received emotion into her, until her body shook with the horror of it.

She couldn't stand by and simply let them all be slaughtered. But what could she do?

Mother and Connall were still hopelessly out of reach, trapped in their own cells in that huge box of a castle in the centre of the crowded city. From her hilltop, Cordelia could glimpse small figures pacing around high stone turrets – archers waiting impatiently for the oncoming battle to spill, inevitably, through the city walls.

'All right then,' said Rosalind. She drew her sword from the sheath that she'd made for herself across their journey.

'Wait, wait, wait. Let me think!' Giles jittered in place, eyes wide and fingers tapping a desperate rhythm against his side. 'This can still work if we change the plan. Instead of all of us sneaking in, Cordy can shift into a bird while the two of us wait right here. Then she'll fly over everything else to get to Mother—'

'And get herself shot down by arrows?' Exasperation leaked from Rosalind's voice as she rocked to a halt, her sword still gripped tightly. 'Can't you see how nervous those archers are? They're only waiting for an excuse to let fly at anything that moves.'

'Then she'll turn into a bug instead! Something so small no one will ever notice—'

'And she'll reach Mother's cell in a week.' Rosalind shook her head impatiently. 'It doesn't matter what kind of animal you choose, Giles. I know you hate the idea of fighting, but if all Cordy had to do was change shape to save Mother and Connall by herself, do you really think she'd still be standing here with the two of us?'

Giles slumped in place, letting out a low sigh of surrender.

Cordelia wrapped her arms tightly around her trembling body, trying to focus through the waves of received panic washing over her and the turmoil of her own emotions. 'I wouldn't just leave you two behind without talking it over first,' she muttered. 'Not any more.'

'Hmmph,' said Rosalind.

Giles's ginger eyebrows rose meaningfully.

'It's true!' She'd learned that lesson at Raven's Nest, and in the long, painful days beforehand. Secrets had nearly destroyed her family. She had promised herself never to keep them any more.

She had also promised herself never to take her triplets for granted again … even at moments like this one, when they gave each other looks so annoying that they practically *deserved* to be abandoned.

'I'm not leaving anyone behind,' she said more steadily, 'but we have to win this battle for everyone's sake – and it'll take all three of us together.'

'To get Mother out of that awful collar?' Giles asked.

'Oh, no.' Rosalind's lips curved into a fierce smile as she met her sister's eyes and started back towards them. '*That's* not the battle she's talking about now. Is it, Cordy?'

'But—'

'We will get Mother out,' Cordelia promised, 'and we'll free Connall and Alys too. But they're not the only ones who need us now.' Taking a deep, shuddering breath, she loosened her arms and pointed at the stone walls beyond the sea of soldiers. 'That city is full of people like the ones we met outside our forest. They have nothing to do with this stupid war! But they're going to be killed by it anyway, and the land is going to be hurt even more badly – unless we do something to stop it, *now*.'

'Us?' Giles demanded. 'How can *we* stop both those armies? Didn't you even watch the spirits' vision at Raven's Nest? I know the land wants you to be its queen, but this war has been going on for *decades*, Cordy. Everyone says it'll never end until the crown is fixed, and that crown is still in pieces after everything we've tried. If they figure out who we are while it's still broken, they'll kill us before we can even try again! Do you really want the three of us to sacrifice our lives for no good reason?'

Sacrifice …

The word chimed like a bell, resonating deep under her feet with all the fractured pieces of the land.

A *true sacrifice …*

Cordelia caught her breath, her head spinning.

Of course! She finally understood. No wonder they hadn't managed to put the crown together in any of their attempts. They'd been missing the most important element.

It was so simple … and so terrifying.

Her teeth started to chatter. She clenched them together.

She couldn't do it. She couldn't bear it!

But the Raven Crown hadn't been formed by the land and its people each pursuing their own paths. It had been sealed by true sacrifices made on both sides. *That* meant giving up something she loved – and Cordelia had learned, across their terrible journey, exactly what and whom she loved too much to ever sacrifice.

That left only one possibility.

'I can do this,' she breathed as shivers rippled through her. 'We all can. We *will*, because no one else – *no one* – is going to die on this land today.'

That was worth any sacrifice.

Cordelia took a deep breath, lowered her chin, and braced herself against the ground. Grass prickled against her ankles. Deeper down – deeper – deeper—

'What are you doing?' Giles demanded. 'Your eyes—'

'Shh!' Rosalind hissed. 'Can't you tell? She's working.'

'Is she?' he asked. 'Or is the land working *through* her? I'm not sure—'

'**We have waited long enough**.' Cordelia's voice resonated with the full weight of Corvenne as her chin rose, drawing its gathered power through her. Echoes rippled down the hillside like an avalanche. The ground in the valley below gave a convulsive shake, sending every soldier stumbling to their knees. Screams sounded behind the city walls …

And Cordelia and the land spoke in unison, their words rolling down the hill like thunder:

'**It is time**.'

23

Time to heal what has been broken.
Time to make things right.

Cordelia's body moved down the long hill, flanked by her triplets. At least, she thought it did. It all seemed very far away. Her vision was blurred with memories not her own, flashing past in uncontrollable succession. Every part of the fractured land was shouting at her at once, sending her visions of past horrors and past promises.

Her right foot slipped beneath her on the dirt path …

Rosalind grabbed her closest arm and pulled her upright. The shock of contact cleared Cordelia's vision for just a moment.

The mass of soldiers in the barren field below was rippling like an agitated swarm of bees, both armies reassembling to face the hillside and the three children.

Swords and pikes glinted before them, under the grey and cloudy sky. Beyond the high city walls, Cordelia sensed even more frantic movement taking place.

'Well …' Giles's laugh shivered with nerves. 'At least we have their attention now.'

'Good,' Cordelia said, with an effort. 'It's your turn.'

'My—?'

'Oh, Giles.' Through her blurred vision and the dizzying rush of green power racing through her veins, Cordelia managed a smile for her gangly, rumpled triplet. 'Haven't you always wanted a proper audience?'

'You told all of us you'd sing for kings and queens one day,' said Rosalind. 'Just look at everyone waiting to hear from you now!'

Shoulders hunching, he shook his head. 'They're not waiting for me. I'm not the Raven heir. I'm useless. I—'

'I can't do this without you,' Cordelia said. It was the truth, and she'd finally come to understand it on their journey. 'This only works – all of it – if we do it together.'

Heart. Spirit. Fierce protection.

All the old contracts had finally been renewed in the form of three newborn babies lying together in one cot … and now, it was time to prove it.

'Do you really think *Cordelia's* going to talk them into seeing sense?' Rosalind demanded. 'Have you ever *met* our sister?' She snorted loudly. 'She can shake those high walls to the ground if she likes, or turn into a lion and eat some soldiers. But you're the only one who knows how to *talk* to people.'

It felt good for Cordelia to roll her eyes. It reminded her, for a startling moment of clarity, that she *was* still Cordelia after all, not just a walking, talking vessel for the land around her.

Vessels probably didn't feel so tempted to poke their sisters, hard.

'You're not useless,' she told Giles. 'You have your own powers, and it's time to use them. All of them.'

Giles stared at her for a long moment. Then he straightened. His shoulders pulled back and his chin rose high for the first time in days. 'You're right,' he said as he brushed off his dirty blue doublet. 'You do need me.' His lips stretched into a fierce smile. 'And I have *just* the right song for this moment!'

Rosalind groaned. 'I said *talk*, you—'

'Shh!' Cordelia shook her head, riding waves of dizziness, as Giles stepped forward and drew a familiar deep breath. He threw out his arms in greeting to the staring soldiers below. 'Let him sing first,' she murmured.

Then Giles sang out a high, clear note, and both of them were stunned into utter silence.

That single note sang around the field from a dozen different angles at once, rising up into unearthly harmony.

Giles had grasped full control over his own sorcery in their frantic flight past the soldiers at Mount Corve ... and now, his voice echoed from everywhere at once. It swirled through the landscape, piercing the air with its purity.

Commanding. Inescapable.

Singing the *truth*:

Burned-out houses
Broken land
Where our homes
Should all still stand ...

His words were rich, golden bells that pealed down the hillside, into the city and across the field into every soldier's ear. It was an incredible, overwhelmingly magical performance – and Cordelia recognised his haunting, melancholy tune immediately. It was the same melody he'd hummed for days as they'd travelled through the blasted landscape, witnesses to devastation.

A loud, wet gulp sounded beside her as his song rang out. Cordelia turned and stared as Rosalind wiped a glistening stream of tears off her face.

'Shut up!' Rosalind hissed when she caught Cordelia looking. 'Don't you dare tell him. I just …' She trailed off, brown eyes still suspiciously bright in her reddened face.

She wasn't the only one. A strange hushed silence had fallen over the sea of adult soldiers. As the triplets walked together down the wide dirt path into the valley, the armed men and women ahead watched in open-mouthed awe …

… And Cordelia spotted more than one of them surreptitiously rubbing their own eyes.

The land was listening too. Cordelia felt it tremble, deep at its core, as Giles's voice rose and fell, filled with a pain and yearning that resonated perfectly with the earth below.

His song carried the same message that the land had screamed for decades, desperate for anyone to listen:

Broken. Broken. Broken. Heal us!

Land in pieces
Families lost
So much death
Too high a cost …

A soldier at the front of the line dropped his pike to the ground as he toppled to his knees, scrubbing his fists across his lowered face.

'Up!' His commander's face was screwed tight and angry, her shoulders held martially tight. 'To your feet, man!'

But all around her, dozens of other men and women fell to their knees like broken leaves from autumn trees, dropping their weapons as Giles's song curled in lapping, wistful waves around them.

> There was a time—
> Could come again—
> When our cousins
> Were our friends,
> When the land
> Was ours to tend.
> If fighting stopped
> This all could end …

Soldiers all across the field gave physical starts with the shock of sudden silence as Giles's magically directed voice cut off, leaving them all stranded. His final word still hung in the air, a dissonant note waiting for resolution.

He had left the song, like his message, wide open. Hurting. Begging them:

> Heal us – and stop this madness!

Sobs sounded all the more startling when they came from deep adult voices all across the crowded field; so many different kneeling, weaponless bodies crying out under different flags. The land shivered beneath Cordelia's feet ... but not in protest this time.

It was *gratitude* that rose in a great green surge through the ground and streamed through her veins.

But not everyone had fallen under the spell of Giles's song. All across the field, scattered leaders barked at their weeping subordinates, haranguing them to get back into formation. In the centre of the field, a small group of armoured men and women had gathered together to head purposefully towards the triplets.

'They're the pretenders to our throne!' bellowed a tall, ferocious duchess with a boar on the shield that she raised into the air. 'Don't let them trick you with their mother's magic!'

She had to be the famous Duchess of Solenne, ready to attack them at long last—

But the rest of her words were cut off by a long groaning creak as the massive iron-banded wooden door in the city walls swung open, revealing the Dukes of Arden and Lune within its entryway.

The bearish Duke of Arden strode forward, fully armoured, massive and bristling with weaponry and fury. The Duke of Lune paced beside him, poised and ready, like a lean wolf waiting to leap upon his enemies.

Behind them, with hands locked together by metal cuffs, flanked by two red-robed sorcerers as prison guards …

'Connall!' Giles's powerful voice turned into a squeak, all his sorcery falling away in shock.

'Your Majesties!' cried the Duke of Lune across the field. 'I believe we have a hostage here that you would prefer to see unhurt.'

Rosalind raised her sword with murderous fury, ready to charge through all the hundreds of soldiers who still stood between them and their older brother.

Connall's voice shot into all their heads at once: **Don't listen to him, any of you. Run! Keep yourselves safe!**

Cordelia looked across the crowded field of soldiers at the brother whose long arms had scooped her away from so many dangers in the past. She shook her head at him as the last of her fears fell away. **This time, Connall, it's our turn to protect you**.

She reached into the makeshift sack that she'd carried all the way from Raven's Nest and pulled out the broken pieces of the Raven Crown.

24

Cordelia had worried that people might not recognise the silver shards.

She'd been wrong.

As she pulled out the three heavy pieces, each engraved with delicate starflowers, light pierced the heavy clouds overhead. It wasn't the bright white lens of sunlight; it was a pale, shimmering green spear that caused breaths to catch all over the tumultuous battlefield as it shot down to illuminate the three fragments in her hand.

'The Raven Crown.' Giles's voice bounced across every edge of the field, powered once again by his own sorcery, as he scooped up one of the pieces. It glimmered in that mystical green light, and he held it high for all to see. 'Gifted to my sister on Mount Corve by the spirits of the land, who had held it for her, waiting, all these years.'

There was a moment of awestruck silence … except in Cordelia's head, where Connall's voice shouted frantically, **Cordelia, what have you done?**

Shh, she thought back at him. **Find some faith!**

'Look! It's still broken!' The Duchess of Solenne strode forward across the field, her helmet bristling with angry iron spikes. 'So what if these ragtag children have stolen its pieces for their own ends?' she roared. 'Soldiers, *attack* these pretenders to the throne!'

A cloud of arrows shot across the field, aimed at the three children on the hill.

It was an impossible array for anyone to defeat. They didn't even have a shield to hide behind. Connall's shout of despair rang out across the battlefield and inside Cordelia's head, endless and echoing—

But of course, Rosalind had come to grips with her own sorcery too, when she had claimed her sword at the gates of Mount Corve. Now she flung out her free hand beside Cordelia, and half of those attacking arrows whirled around immediately in mid-flight, flying back over the heads of the soldiers who had shot them. Her long sword cut through the air with incredible speed, slashing all the remaining arrows into splintering pieces that rained harmlessly across the grass.

'Halt. Halt! H*alt!*' The four dukes and the duchess were all bellowing the same word through the chaos – but as the cloud of arrows finally trickled to a stop, leaving the field in even more disarray than before, their own argument only grew louder and fiercer.

'How *dare*—!'

'Be silent—!'

'The *outrage*—!'

'Just *sorcery*—!'

They all gathered together in the centre of the field, screaming and waving their heavily armoured arms in each other's faces, but Cordelia ignored them all to shake her head at Giles. He had made one mistake in his earlier announcement. 'They weren't just holding this crown for *me*,' she said quietly. 'We have to do this *together* to make it work. Remember?'

In her hands, the three pieces had lain perfectly quiet and still.

Now, she passed the final piece to Rosalind, who lowered her sword ... and a low, vibrating hum shivered through each of the broken pieces.

Giles gulped visibly as he turned away from the battlefield, his gaze fixed on the silver buzzing gently in his palm. 'This ... is new. Why didn't it do this any of the other times we tried to mend it?'

'Because I didn't understand, then, what I had to do to seal our part of the bargain,' said Cordelia.

Rosalind squared her shoulders and met Cordelia's gaze, her face still red and glowing from her victory in battle. 'What do you need from the two of us?'

'Heart and fierce protection.' Cordelia took a breath. 'We have to *all* agree to the contract. Together.'

And I'll make the sacrifice to seal it.

She stepped, willingly, towards the triplets she had squabbled with and jostled against all her life.

Her free hand landed on Rosalind's strong shoulder. Giles's long musician's fingers gripped Cordelia's shoulder as Rosalind's free hand landed on his.

'We swear,' Cordelia said, and the others repeated her words as the adult dukes and duchess squabbled obliviously on the field beneath them, 'to love this land and to listen to its needs and to protect it with *all* our skills. We three seal ourselves to the land of Corvenne … forever.'

Together, they set the three pieces of the broken crown in place … and inside her head, Cordelia added one more promise that only the land could hear:

It's all yours now. I'm giving it up for you.

Will you make your own sacrifice for me in return?

A thunderous boom erupted beneath them in deafening answer.

Bright green filled Cordelia's vision.

Pressure filled her ears until they popped.

Everything was noise. Everything was confusion.

Blinded, deafened, Cordelia gripped Rosalind's shoulder for dear life. Giles's grip held her in place.

Behind and around them, a thousand voices sang in chorus:

You are ours.
We are yours.
Forever and ever in endless harmony.
Together.
Unified.
Three in one.
Home!

'Cordy. Cordy! *Cordy!*' Giles and Rosalind were both shouting at once, their words breaking through the triumphant song of the land.

Cordelia blinked hard, swallowing again and again as she tried to break through to reach them – so close but so entirely untouchable. Green stems filled her veins, bursting into joyful blossom. The mountains around her were her steady guardians, anchoring her in place. The—

'*Cordy!*'

Giles's face swam into focus before her, and she came back into herself with a jolt.

Tears streamed down his grimy cheeks, but his smile was full of joy. 'We did it! Look!'

It seemed to take an eon to relocate herself in her too-small, limited body and to take control of all its different pieces. But once she finally managed to move her chin down ...

The Raven Crown glowed in the triplets' three hands, heavy, silver ... and without a single mark along its shining curves to show where it had ever been broken.

Green light surrounded all three of them in a beaming circle underneath a beautifully sunny, cloudless sky.

Leafy birch, ash and oak trees – vast and whispering – had erupted to march behind them, turning the path down the hillside into a thick, vibrant woodland.

Before them, joyful starflowers covered the grass of what had once been a battlefield. Weapons lay scattered, abandoned, among the bright white blossoms.

All across the starflower field, figures knelt now in their hundreds.

... Every one of them paying deference to her.

The Dukes of Arden and Lune were among them. The other dukes were kneeling too, and so was the Duchess of

Solenne, her spiked helmet discarded on the grass nearby, and her rebellion at an end.

Only Connall still stood at the far end of the field, staring at all those prone bodies with a lost, stunned look … but as his gaze finally rose to meet hers, he too sank down to his knees beside the two sorcerers who had guarded him.

I've found that faith, he whispered in her head, voice full of wonder. **I should have known that you'd dare anything, my wildest little sister. But oh, Cordelia, what have you sacrificed for our sakes?**

'There's no denying it now!' Rosalind raised the Raven Crown and set it firmly on Cordelia's head. It fit there with supernatural precision. 'You *are* the true Raven Queen for good, whether anyone else likes it or not.'

Giles nodded enthusiastically, leaning in to admire the crown on her head. 'No one can pretend they have a better claim to the throne – so *no one* can change what you are from now on!'

'No. No one ever can,' Cordelia echoed, her voice eerily distant in her own ears. *Not even me.*

The crown bore down on her head with far more weight than those three sealed shards could account for on their own. The rustle of surrendered falling wings inside her body was too faint for anyone else to hear.

Would it fade away completely, in time? Or would she hear its echo haunting her forever?

Her human feet were heavy and solid on the earth, anchored by the crown she wore. Invisible green roots held her down almost as tightly as the trees of the brand-new forest in her wake. She had sealed her spirit to the land, it had grounded her and swallowed her into lifelong service as the true Queen of Corvenne …

And she had promised away her own magic to seal the crown. She would never be able to change her shape again.

Far too soon, every duke and duchess on the field was striding towards the triplets ahead of a jostling crowd of followers.

'Your Majesty.' The Duke of Lune swept a low bow to Cordelia as the Duchess of Solenne hurried to catch up with him, the three other dukes wrestling for position behind them. 'I am delighted to reunite you with your brother at last! As your loyal regents, Arden and I will of course be—'

'*No.*'

The land and its spirits had made their own sacrifice to mend the Raven Crown, giving up to Cordelia as much as she had given up to them. Now, all their vast green power lay in *Cordelia's* control, just as it had for the Raven kings and queens of old … and she would never be anyone's helpless pawn again.

'I'm not having any *regents*, and you're not taking control of this kingdom.' Spiky bushes of thorns erupted from the grass around her as Cordelia stalked forward in her bloodstained old green linen gown, the earth rumbling underneath the dukes' and duchess's feet. 'You *will* release Connall from those cuffs right now,' she snarled, 'free Alys from wherever you've put her, and *take off* that horrible collar from my mother, or I'll *pull down that castle* to do it myself!'

'She can,' Rosalind told them, 'and she will. But even if she didn't …' She lifted her square chin proudly. '*I'd* get Mother free with my sword, no matter how many soldiers stood against me!' The memory of victory rang in her voice, until Cordelia could almost see the remnants of those shattered arrows before them.

'Actually,' said Giles firmly, 'we would do it together. Our family will never be separated again. Not by *anybody*. We will *all* be safe and respected in my sister's court.'

Every duke and duchess opened their mouth at once to argue … but the ground leaped up beneath them before they could utter a word and tipped them all into obedient bows.

As they reluctantly lowered their heads in acceptance, Giles's best performing smile broke across his face. 'Excellent,' he said. 'Now you may all lead us to our mother.'

25

It took an absurdly long argument before Cordelia could finally start up the circular staircase to the castle tower where Mother had been imprisoned. The dukes – Arden and Lune in particular – were adamant that, as queen, Cordelia should sit in state in the grand throne room and wait for Mother to be summoned to her side. Nothing that any of the children said made any difference – until Rosalind finally cut through all their bluster.

'Don't waste any more of your breath,' she snapped. 'We already know *exactly* how the two of you have kept her, so there's no point in trying to hide the ugly details. The three of us saw her in that prison cell days ago.'

'You … did?' Lune's eyebrows shot up.

The Duchess of Solenne looked smug.

Arden's face reddened with furious chagrin.

The sidelong looks that they all gave each other were anything but reassuring.

At least the dark and gloomy stairwell that led up to Mother's tower was too narrow to fit the whole entourage that had marched the siblings through the town. It took Giles's smooth tongue to persuade the Duchess of Solenne and her two allies to stop at the bottom of the stairs. When Cordelia reached the locked and ironbound door at the very highest level of the tower, she turned to Lune and Arden with her jaw firmly set.

'Pass me the key.'

'Your Majesty, we would be more than happy to—'

'**The key**,' she snapped, infusing her voice with the full power of the land far below her feet.

She had endured everything else today. She had accepted the anchor of the Raven Crown. She had given up her wings for the sake of the kingdom and everyone inside it, and she had stepped voluntarily into this cage of a stone castle.

But she *would not* face her mother at long last with these two dukes as interested onlookers. It was too much to ask.

The Duke of Arden opened his mouth to object. The Duke of Lune stilled him with a swift headshake. 'Of course,' he said smoothly, 'you'll want a moment of privacy. We'll wait out here, for your convenience.'

Cordelia turned the key in the lock with shaking fingers ... and then stepped back to let Giles and Rosalind rush in first.

She slipped into the shadowy room behind them and Connall, closing the door firmly behind her and keeping the big iron key clenched tightly in her fist. Her eyes stayed fixed on the dirty stone floor while her triplets flung themselves into their mother's startled embrace.

'Rosalind? Giles? What are you two doing here? They haven't caught you too—? *Oh!*' Mother's voice cut off with a gasp.

A heavy weight seemed to press down against Cordelia's head, far heavier than the silver crown she wore. She pushed back against it, forcing her chin upright and her gaze forward ... to find her mother staring at her over her triplets' heads with an expression of undiluted horror.

Connall silently closed one hand in support around her shoulder ... and Cordelia's spine stiffened with the strength of that connection. 'We're here to rescue you, Mother.' Her voice was perfectly steady as she raised her chin an extra notch. 'Aren't you glad?'

'Have you gone mad?' Eyes wide and haunted, Mother shook her head desperately. 'This throne will kill you, Cordelia. I *told* you! If I could ever, just once, trust you to *listen* and *do as I say* instead of wildly running off and ignoring all my—'

'Mother,' said Connall, 'look at the crown Cordelia's wearing. Please. See *exactly* what she's wearing now!'

Mother frowned and squinted through the shadows. Shoulders squared, Cordelia stepped closer to catch the slanting bars of dim light that fell from the high window.

Mother let out a small, incoherent, broken noise. Then she swallowed hard. 'But … how—?'

'Oh, we'll tell you everything,' Giles said cheerfully. 'Don't worry! I'm working on a song *all* about it.'

'Make sure you remember to include all the juicy details from my battles – both of them!' Rosalind patted the long sword that hung by her side, and Mother's eyes widened even more at the sight of it.

'But – the danger—!'

'We don't have to hide any more,' Connall said. 'Cordelia's changed everything for us.'

'We *will* tell you all about it,' Cordelia promised, 'and we'll get that horrible collar off you too. But, Mother …'

She took a deep breath as she met her mother's fierce, dark gaze – so familiar, so infuriating and so beloved that her whole body trembled with its impact. The weight of her mother's shock and disapproval was almost enough to topple her completely.

But Mother wasn't all-powerful and all-knowing, as Cordelia had once believed her to be.

She was fallible. She made mistakes. She had her own weaknesses, like everybody else.

And her love, fierce and unyielding across the years, had made all of them a family.

'I *am* the Raven Queen,' Cordelia said, 'whether you like it or not. I won't always do as you wish from now on, and you can't give me orders any more.'

'Cordelia …' Mother started forward, frowning – but Cordelia's raised hand halted her in mid-step.

'I promise, I will always listen to your advice – but you *cannot* keep any more secrets from us, no matter who you're trying to protect! I know it can feel too dangerous to share them. I've made that mistake now too. But the truth is, it nearly ruined everything … and we need to be able to trust *you*.'

At Cordelia's final words, Mother flinched. She looked down at Giles and Rosalind for support.

Even Giles didn't stand up for her this time, though. Cordelia's triplets both stepped back and looked up at Mother steadily, waiting for her reply. Connall stood by Cordelia's side.

When their mother finally spoke, her voice was hoarse with emotion. 'I have only ever tried to protect you all.'

'We know,' Giles said.

Rosalind nodded.

'We'll protect you too,' said Cordelia. 'But you have to understand that things have changed. If you can't – if you hate the throne too much – then you can go back to our forest and stay there. I promise, I won't stop you. No one else will, either. You'll be perfectly safe there forever.'

Mother shook her head, moistening her lips. 'You know I would never abandon any of my children,' she whispered. 'You *must* all know that by now. I love all of you.'

'We love you too.' Cordelia's throat tightened.

'Then …' Mother blinked rapidly. 'You'll let me stay? And I'll find a way to accept your throne, somehow?'

'We both will,' Cordelia promised.

The strong stone walls seemed to close in around them with her words … and something shattered in Cordelia's chest.

It was the wall that she had built with all her strength to hide away from the truth of her surrendered wings and everything else she had gone through ever since that first night in the forest when she had flown out of their castle and lost her first home for good.

She had stayed so strong behind that wall for so long.

She had tried so hard not to cry.

But when Mother tentatively held out her arms, Cordelia ran straight into them … and the tears that streamed out of her face to soak into her mother's warm, familiar chest felt like rain falling on to barren earth, bringing the whole parched land back to life.

Two days later, the long, curving high street through Corvenne's capital city was crowded unbearably full of people. How could so many human beings ever have squeezed into one place?

Flowers rained down from the windows of the tall, skinny white buildings, latticed in black beams, that leaned out over the street. If Cordelia could only have slipped into bird form, she would have shot through that shower of blooms and arrived at the grand Hall of Investiture in less than five minutes. Instead, she was paraded at a snail's pace down the street between her siblings with all five adult dukes blocking them in, walking before and behind the family with serene, unhurried smiles.

Rows of soldiers acted as human shields around them while a massive crowd of shouting, singing onlookers fought to shove through all those lines of protection, hands desperately outstretched to grasp at Cordelia through the deafeningly loud confusion. Mother and Alys were waiting ahead, making a final check for safety before the ceremony of investiture could begin.

The sickly-sweet stench of so many sweaty strangers mixed in Cordelia's shallow breaths with the horrible raw stink of human waste from the open gutters that ran down the cobblestoned street. The Raven Crown pressed into her scalp, painfully heavy. Impossible to remove in front of everyone.

She was hemmed in on every side. She was trapped. No space to move – no clean air to breathe—

Rosalind's hand closed around her elbow. 'Chin up,' her sister whispered into her ear. 'Remember, you're their queen now. They just want a good look, to know who to thank for saving all their lives when you stopped that endless war.'

Cordelia couldn't answer. She had to keep her jaw clamped shut or else her teeth would start chattering in front of everyone.

You promised, she reminded herself fiercely. *You promised.*

Connall frowned down at her from his position at the end of their row, his hands freed once more, and his voice grave in her head. **You're safe now, little sister**.

So are you, she thought back to him.

He was a beloved brother of the true Raven Queen and the newly named Duke of Harcourt too, as Cordelia had passed that title to him. The land itself had swallowed up their grandmother; no one else would ever dare try to imprison him again. For the first time in his life, her older brother could relax his guard.

Cordelia couldn't open her mouth to say it, though.

Beside her, Giles took one swift look down at her tightly clenched face and then said, 'Did I tell you three that I've thought up a new song? It's going to be my best one ever, I'm certain.'

'Already?' Rosalind groaned. 'I don't know if I'm ready yet for another—'

'Oh, this one is far more epic than my last,' he said cheerfully. 'You see, it's all about the really itchy, grimy bits between my toes and how much they've been bothering me these last few days of travel. It's a follow-up to my stomach song but *far* more tragic and impressive. Here, listen!'

He sucked in a loud, deep breath, then clasped his hands to his heart as he launched into a piercing falsetto that soared like a cat's yowl through all the din:

My toes! My toes!
They smell nothing like a—

'Shush!' Rosalind snorted with laughter as she gestured menacingly at him. 'D'you want these people to start throwing water instead of flowers, just to shut you up?'

At the end of their row, serious Connall looked indescribably pained by his younger siblings' antics. Giles beamed, though, as he glanced down at the small smile that Cordelia hadn't managed to suppress. Her teeth weren't even trying to chatter any more.

'Cordy likes my song,' he said smugly, 'and I think everyone in Corvenne will be singing it within a week at most. How could they resist? I haven't even sung you all the best bit yet. You'll never guess what I came up with as a rhyme for *toe hair*—'

'Stop!' Rosalind clapped her hands to her ears. 'I am begging you!'

But of course, there was never any stopping Giles once he'd fully launched into a performance. By the time they reached the next turning of the street, Cordelia's chest was quaking with barely suppressed laughter, and the overwhelming din of the grasping crowd around her had settled into a dull roar. Even the crown didn't feel quite so heavy any more. It *was* hers, after all – and all the people she loved would help her to grow into it.

The whole land of Corvenne stretched around her now, vast and open to all her exploring senses.

She was the Raven Queen – and with her family by her side, she was ready to rule.

~The End~

ACKNOWLEDGEMENTS

I am so grateful to Ellen Holgate and Lucy Mackay-Sim at Bloomsbury Children's Books for supporting me and my work and pushing me to aim higher and higher every time with your thoughtful edits and incisive questions. My books are so much better because of both of you! And thank you so much to my agent, Molly Ker Hawn, for being the best partner in publishing that I could ever imagine. I'm so lucky to be able to call my agent a friend.

Thank you to Jenn Reese, Patrick Samphire, Aliette de Bodard, Dave Burgis, Rene Sears and Jamie Samphire for beta-reading chapters as I wrote them at various stages of this process. Thank you to Rene Sears, Aliette de Bodard, Ben Burgis and David Burgis for giving me fantastic feedback on the first chapters and proposal for this book, and to Claire Fayers and Patrick Samphire for wonderful critiques of the full first draft.

Thank you to Beatrice Cross, Jade Westwood and Grace

Ball for marketing and publicity, to Veronica Lyons for careful copy-editing, to Eugenie Woodhouse for proof-reading, to Fliss Stevens for managing the production process so beautifully, to Jet Purdie for the cover design and gorgeous chapter headers, and to Pétur Antonsson for the beautiful cover illustration.

Thank you to Jamie and Ollie Samphire for illustrating my hard-copy manuscript with perfect, thoughtful drawings that gave me inspiration as I wrote and for sharing so many wonderful conversations with me about what animals we would all turn into if we had Cordelia's powers.

Thank you to Tricia Sullivan for putting me up and feeding me homemade chocolate-chip cookies while I wrestled my way through a difficult part of the first draft. Thank you to Patrick Samphire, Y.S. Lee and Tiffany Trent for a wonderful, nourishing writing retreat that helped me make so much progress on my manuscript, and thank you to my parents for the generous childcare that made that retreat possible.

Thank you so much to everyone on Facebook who answered my bat-signal (bird-signal?) and gave me fantastic suggestions on the birds that Cordelia would see and/or hear in her woods: Sorrel Jones, Lindsay Glasspool, Kathy Burgis, Freda Warrington, Sarah Pitt, Katya Coupland, Cecilia Busby, Ashley and Alexandra Roumbas Goldstein, Nicky Hopkins,

Dave Chetwynd, Elizabeth Williamson, Teryn Raptor Dear, Helen Hall, Matt Daubney, and Stephanie Maurer Whelan and her Terry Pratchett group.

(PS: Any mistakes that I've made anyway are entirely my own!)

Thank you to all my Slack and private Facebook group colleagues for moral support, cheering-on, pen and ink recommendations, and company along the way. It made a huge difference!

Thank you so much to my brothers, Ben and David Burgis, for moral support along the way. There's a reason why I write so many siblings into my books! We may live in different parts of the world nowadays – and there may be times when we've squabbled every bit as much as the triplets in this novel! – but when it's the middle of the night and I'm scared, you are always the first ones I think to reach out to, because I know that the three of us are a lifelong team – and that means the world to me.

And thank you so much to my parents, Richard and Kathy Burgis, for teaching me what family means and providing me with so much love and support even when we're separated by an ocean. I have been so lucky with my family.

THE
RAVEN
HEIR
QUIZ

Which Animal Are You?

Imagine you had Cordelia's powers and could turn into any animal you chose! Would you be happiest running through the forest on four paws, spreading your wings and flying, or perhaps just having a snooze in the sun? Find your perfect animal form by taking the quiz!

1 Your parents announce that you and *all* your relatives – grandparents, cousins, uncles and aunts – will be staying together at a holiday camp for a full week of non-stop family bonding. How do you react?

a. Hooray! I always feel happiest and most relaxed when I'm surrounded by my family's love.

b. Noooooooooooooooooooooooooooooooooooo ooooooooooooooo!!!!!!!!!!!

c. Sorry, that's just too many family members for me. I'm only comfortable hanging out with small groups, so I'll be sneaking out before the distant relatives arrive.

d. I don't mind gathering with that many relatives if it's a real emergency, but if it isn't, I would rather not go.

e. Can I spend some of the time with the whole family and the rest of the time relaxing on my own? I do love my family, but I also need space to breathe!

2 A mysterious parcel arrives by post, addressed to you – but before you can open it (or even see the return address), your parents swoop in and hide the parcel away, saying: 'Shh. That's for later!' How do you react?

a. I'll work with my siblings to hunt it down together and we'll have fun on the way.

b. I'll stubbornly follow every clue to track it down myself and investigate the parcel from every angle, no matter how much chaos I cause along the way or what anyone else thinks about it.

c. I'll sneak quietly through the house to find it. No one will even know I've been there.

d. I'll problem-solve by figuring out which strategy is most likely to succeed – searching for it myself, tricking my parents into revealing the location, or talking a friend or two into helping out.

e. I'll tirelessly stalk my parents through the house, repeating, 'Tell me – tell me where it is!' until they finally give up and reveal its whereabouts.

3 You're daydreaming about your perfect day and exactly how you'd like to spend it. Which of these sounds best?

  a. I'll spend the day hanging out with my whole family, playing around together and going on fun adventures.

  b. I'll explore a beautiful place all by myself, investigating everything interesting that I see.

  c. I'll successfully sneak into somewhere I've always wanted to visit but have never been allowed to.

  d. I'll design my own game and play it either alone or with my best friend.

  e. I'll lounge in a beautifully sunny spot and dream the day away.

4 Which of these would be your worst nightmare?

  a. Being stuck horribly alone for ever and ever and … !

  b. Being surrounded by other people, with no space to breathe and no time to think on my own. Aargh!

  c. Standing onstage with everyone staring at me. Being the centre of attention feels incredibly unsafe!

d. Having my most precious belongings stolen from me.

e. Being startled again and again by loud banging noises that make it impossible to enjoy my daily nap.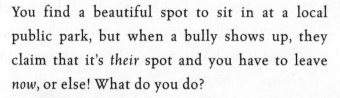

5 You find a beautiful spot to sit in at a local public park, but when a bully shows up, they claim that it's *their* spot and you have to leave *now*, or else! What do you do?

a. Well, of course, I'll already be hanging out in a group with at least a few of my friends or relatives, so we'll immediately take on that jerk together and teach them *never* to threaten any of us again!

b. When I get mad, I get really *scary*-mad. After I explode at that fool, they'll never dare make such ridiculous threats again.

c. Run! I know I'm not a fighter, so it's only sensible to listen to the warning and get away in time to stay safe.

d. I'll leave for the moment, but then I'll gather up all my friends from their own houses and we'll take him on together. We may not spend our whole lives in each other's pockets, but we always work together when we're needed.

e. I'll never let them see that I'm scared, because I have far too much pride. If I actually think I can win, I'll stay and fight. But if I can see that that would be a losing battle, I'll just say something really sarcastic and scathing and then walk away with my head held high.

ANSWERS

MOSTLY A: You're a wolf!

Wolves are natural pack animals who work best as a team and love playing as well as hunting together. You'll have the best time running and singing with your pack across forests or fields as a beautiful, loyal wolf.

MOSTLY B: You're a bear!

You value peace and quiet and enjoy your alone time in the deep forest. Generally you're pretty peaceful, but if you get angry, you get *really* angry. You'll be happiest as a brave, determined bear, living life on exactly your own terms.

MOSTLY C: You're a mouse!

People tend to overlook mice, but that's actually their superpower. It's almost impossible to keep them from sneaking anywhere they want to get exactly what they need! You're naturally inquisitive and have a true gift for spy-work. You'll be happiest as a tiny, stealthy mouse, using your size and your cleverness to your best advantage.

MOSTLY D: You're a raven!

Ravens are incredibly smart problem-solvers who come up with brilliant strategies for solving even the most challenging puzzles, and also love coming up with new games, whether they end up playing those games alone or with a friend. You're usually happy to be on your own, following your own interests and working on your own projects, but you're always ready to help your friends or your relatives when they really need you, and you know that they'll always have your back as well. You'll be happiest soaring through the sky as a raven, charting your own adventures.

MOSTLY E: You're a cat!

You're curious and playful and you love spending time with the people you love most, but you're also wonderfully independent, and you need plenty of quiet time on your own. Luckily you're fantastically adaptable to all sorts of different situations, and even when you get a little grouchy from time to time, people will still enjoy having you around. You'll love pouncing and stalking and just purring in the sun as a delightfully unique cat.

ABOUT THE AUTHOR

Stephanie Burgis grew up in a big, noisy, loving family in Michigan, USA. These days she is a dual citizen of the US and the UK and lives in South Wales (land of dragons) with her husband, the author Patrick Samphire, and their children. She loves to write books about history, magic, families, bravery, dragons and chocolate! *The Raven Heir* is Stephanie's fourth book for Bloomsbury.

Three magical adventures about acceptance, family, friendship – and dragons!

Read the whole series ...

AVAILABLE NOW

Prim and proper nineteenth-century England is definitely not the place for magic . . . but that's not going to stop Kat Stephenson!

Join Kat in her Improper Adventures today . . .